JAMES BARTLEMAN

A MATTER OF CONSCIENCE

DUNDURN
A J. PATRICK BOYER BOOK
TORONTO

Cover image: 123RF.com/serezniy
Printer: Webcom

Library and Archives Canada Cataloguing in Publication

Bartleman, James, 1939-, author
    A matter of conscience / James Bartleman.

(A J. Patrick Boyer book)
Issued in print and electronic formats.
ISBN 978-1-4597-4112-6 (softcover).--ISBN 978-1-4597-4113-3 (PDF).--
ISBN 978-1-4597-4114-0 (EPUB)

    I. Title.

PS8603.A783M38 2018   C813'.6   C2017-905865-7
                                      C2017-905866-5

1 2 3 4 5   22 21 20 19 18

We acknowledge the support of the **Canada Council for the Arts**, which last year invested $153 million to bring the arts to Canadians throughout the country, and the **Ontario Arts Council** for our publishing program. We also acknowledge the financial support of the **Government of Ontario**, through the **Ontario Book Publishing Tax Credit** and the **Ontario Media Development Corporation**, and the **Government of Canada**.

Nous remercions le **Conseil des arts du Canada** de son soutien. L'an dernier, le Conseil a investi 153 millions de dollars pour mettre de l'art dans la vie des Canadiennes et des Canadiens de tout le pays.

Care has been taken to trace the ownership of copyright material used in this book. The author and the publisher welcome any information enabling them to rectify any references or credits in subsequent editions.

— *J. Kirk Howard, President*

The publisher is not responsible for websites or their content unless they are owned by the publisher.

Printed and bound in Canada.

VISIT US AT

🐚 dundurn.com | 🐦 @dundurnpress | 📘 dundurnpress | 📷 dundurnpress

Dundurn
3 Church Street, Suite 500
Toronto, Ontario, Canada
M5E 1M2

Dedicated to the murdered, disappeared, and abused
Indigenous women and girls of Canada

CONTENTS

ABOUT THIS BOOK

A Matter of Conscience is a work of fiction, the characters are fictional, and the views they express don't necessarily reflect those of the author. The Yellow Dog First Nation, the South Caribou First Nation, the Wolverine First Nation, the town of Murdoch, the Amalgamated Wawatay Cree Tribal Council, the Calvin Mine, the Northern Lights Bar and Grill, and the Desolation River don't exist.

Descriptions of identity used by First Peoples have evolved over the years. First Nation people were described in the *Indian Act* of 1876 as Indians, a term that was once generally accepted among First Nation people themselves. For example, the author's late mother and her contemporaries at the Chippewas of Rama First Nation were proud to call themselves Indian, though it has fallen out of favour today. In this book, the author refers to specific linguistic and cultural groups such as Mohawk, Ojibwa, Cree, Métis, Indian, First Nation, Native, Aboriginal, and Indigenous according to context and time frame.

Many people rely on novels to obtain their knowledge and insights on the challenges facing Indigenous peoples in Canada today. For that reason, the author has included a section of key documents for readers to consult should they wish to dig deeper into the issues raised in his short novel.

PREFACE

My mother, Maureen Benson Bartleman, might have become a murdered or missing Indigenous woman. She grew up on the Chippewas of Rama Indian Reserve, now Chippewas of Rama First Nation, in an abusive household filled with violent quarrels between her parents and marked by beatings from her mother and grandmother. When she was thirteen, her parents' marriage collapsed. Relatives on the reserve took in three siblings, and a family at Moose Deer Point Indian Reserve adopted a fourth child. My mother was cut loose to find her way to nearby Orillia where she met my father, a white man. He was a carefree eighteen-year-old labourer who had dropped out of school in Grade 4 to ride the rails across Canada, looking for work during the Great Depression.

She fudged her age on the licence, and they married. My father took her to meet his parents and siblings who welcomed her and gave her the love she had never received at home. The marriage would be a good and stable one, lasting sixty-eight years before my father died. My mother died at the Getsidjig Endaawaad extended-care facility on the reserve at the age of ninety, never having fully overcome the trauma of childhood abuse and adolescent abandonment made worse by thoughts of what her life might have been if she hadn't met my father.

I followed the cascading reports of murdered and missing Indigenous women over the years with growing dismay. I had come to writing late in life but had already written several novels with Indigenous themes, including *The Redemption of Oscar Wolf* from the perspective of a First Nation person confronting the challenges of being Indian in mid-twentieth-century Canada. I set out to do the same about Murdered and Missing Indigenous Women and victims of the Sixties Scoop. My goal was to penetrate the anonymity of dry statistics to explore in the form of a novel why society doesn't care about these women and girls, why people avert their eyes when faced with the suicide of Indigenous but not white children, and why Canadians in general are more prepared to help the poor of the Third World than the First Peoples in their own country — to the extent that such aberrant behaviours can ever be explained.

I have never forgotten the discrimination my family encountered when I was growing up in a white village in Muskoka in the 1940s. Since my mother had married a white man, she had lost her status as a Treaty Indian and we couldn't live on her home reserve. Because we were an Aboriginal family, the people of the village didn't fully accept us, at least in the beginning. I will never forget local teenagers calling my mother racial epithets so terrible I can't include them in a novel. I will never forget the poverty of those early years, coming home from school one day to find my mother had been forced to put down my dog because she didn't have the money to pay for a tag. We were still crying fifty years later. The desperate poverty of my grandfather, blind and sick and waiting to die back on the reserve, remains seared in my memory.

But I also saw that tragedy wasn't restricted to Indigenous people. I remember the wave of suicides by villagers escaping unpayable debt loads and unhappy marriages that cast a pall over those years. I remember the wife-beating among our neighbours, driving the wives to seek temporary refuge with our family in our old house as the village constable tried to talk sense into their husbands.

I also wanted to explore in my novel the complexities of Indigenous racial identity. I hadn't given the matter much thought until I was eight or nine when my otherwise colour-blind father told me, after I had let him down on some matter of no account, that if I wasn't careful, I would grow up to be a shiftless Indian. This made me speechless with a rage mixed with helplessness. The rage came from a profound feeling that he was being profoundly disrespectful to my mother, my brother, my sisters, me, and all Indians. The helplessness came from the seed he planted in my mind that my life was predestined to failure because of the Indian blood in my veins.

With my light-coloured skin, I could have dealt with the problem by pretending to be white when I left the village for good, but that would have betrayed my family and been hypocritical. I thus embraced the Indian side of my identity, speaking up when others made racist comments about Indians in my presence, whether from colleagues in the staff room in the school where I taught before I joined the foreign service, from public service colleagues, from an elected member of the Yukon government during a briefing I attended in Whitehorse, even from black South African senior officials who should have known better when I was high commissioner in Pretoria.

One of the proudest days of my life was when the unjust provision of the *Indian Act* denying rights to the children of Indian mothers and white men was changed. With my mother, brother, and sisters, I was granted Indian status and recognized as a member of the Chippewas of Rama First Nation, with the right to live there if I wanted. When I was accepted as one of theirs by my mother's people, one of the great ambiguities of my identity was settled, and I was free to participate as a legitimate Indigenous member of Canada's multinational (English-speaking, French-speaking, and Indigenous) country.

PART I

BRENDA
1972–1990

The measure of any society is how it treats its women and girls.

— MICHELLE OBAMA

I

THE BABY SCOOPERS

In the summer of 1972, a Government of Ontario float plane landed on the Albany River flowing through the Yellow Dog Indian Reserve in northwestern Ontario. Word quickly spread throughout the community: "The baby scoopers are back!" Fathers and mothers dropped what they were doing and hurried to pick up and hide their infants, but it was too late. The resident Indian agent, Steve Caruthers, had already skulked about and drawn up a list of babies to be removed without telling the parents. He was now driving his government van with Johnny Powell, a baby-faced RCMP constable in full and intimidating uniform and armed with a service revolver and truncheon, beside him on the passenger seat. Hilda White, a nurse wearing a well-pressed, prim, and starched white uniform, and Louise Bacon, a bewildered social worker from the Children's Aid Society headquarters in Toronto, sat behind them on the second row. The seats on the third row had been removed, and the space was occupied by five bassinets equipped with sheets and blankets.

At the first cabin, the home of Maria and Isaac Makwa, Steve pushed open the door without knocking and went in, beckoning the others to follow. A young couple, no more than sixteen years old, were eating their breakfast, and their six-month-old twin babies were in cradleboards beside them.

"We've come for your children," Steve announced. Pointing to Johnny, who reacted by lowering his head and shifting his weight from one foot to the other, he added, "This officer of the law will arrest you if you make any trouble." Turning to Hilda and Louise, who glanced at each other uneasily, he said, "These two ladies are from the Children's Aid Society and will take the babies to Toronto. Is everything clear so far?"

The Makwas said nothing. They had spent most of their lives in a residential school where they had been taught to obey the edicts of white teachers and officials without question under penalty of receiving a sharp slap across the face.

Steve carefully extracted a prepared statement from his briefcase and read it slowly, enunciating each word with careful precision. "It is my duty to inform you, Maria Makwa, and you, Isaac Makwa, that you were seen drinking alcoholic beverages in the recent past by reliable persons, who shall remain unidentified, at the home of a well-known bootlegger, leaving your children unattended, an act of gross neglect. On that basis, and since the neglect of children is not tolerated in Canada, I hereby declare you to be unfit parents. Your children will be immediately removed from your care and transferred to the care of the Ontario welfare authorities to be put up for adoption to couples in Canada or elsewhere who will give them the love and protection they need. Death certificates will be issued, wiping out and destroying any record of their Indian heritage, and they will receive new white identities. The adoptive parents will not be told the origins of the children, and the children will never know the names of the biological parents. To protect the children, the files relating to the case will be sealed, you will never be told where the children will be placed, and you will never see them again. This decision is final and you have no recourse under the law."

The Makwas stared at the floor and remained silent as Hilda and Louise moved in, unfastened the straps holding their babies in place in their cradleboards, pulled their infants free, wrapped them in government-issue blankets, and hurried outside. Steve and Johnny followed closely behind, providing cover for the women and the stolen babies as if they were bank robbers escaping the scene of a crime. The raiding party moved on to the other designated cabins and followed the same routine until the last of the morning's quota was filled. After looking around to see if anyone was coming to stop them, Steve drove his van back to the river where the pilot was keeping the plane's engine turning over slowly, waiting for his passengers and a fast getaway.

As Hilda and Louise carried the babies from the van, Steve told them to hurry — a grieving mother or father, with a grandfather and grandmother in tow, might still come sobbing to reclaim their offspring, and the situation would become messy. "Messiness attracts the attention of the press and is always bad," he often said. The *Indian Act*, or maybe it was just guidelines from the public-relations folks, had apparently said something to that effect about messiness, and that was good enough for Steve.

Steve had been burned early in his career when he opened the door to *his office on his reserve* to find a member of a visiting delegation sitting at *his desk* and using *his telephone* to brief journalists in far-off Toronto on living conditions on *his reserve*. He had brought the conversation to an end in a hurry, but the damage had been done. Headlines indignantly criticizing Indian Affairs for allowing Indians on *his reserve* to live in packing crates, and drink polluted water had been splashed across newspapers, embarrassing the minister. Headquarters had sent him a message dressing him down, telling him he was under no circumstances to allow visitors to speak to the press and to refer all questions to the Indian Affairs press spokesperson, who was an expert at spin. Steve thus had spent his career anxiously keeping members of the press, and for good measure the officials at Indian Affairs headquarters, in the dark about what was happening on the different reserves where he served.

The visiting team lugged the bassinets with their howling babies aboard the plane and laid them down beside a hamper filled with diapers and bottles of baby formula. Someone inside closed the door, the pilot gunned the engine, and Steve took an axe and cut the rope attaching the pontoons to a stump on the shore. The plane leaped ahead into the wind, buffeted its way over the oncoming waves, and slowly rose until it was high above the black spruce bush on the other side of the river.

"We've done God's work today," Hilda shouted above the plane's roar and the screams of the babies. Louise, who knew Indigenous families would cry that night, wasn't convinced.

Buckled into his seat and staring out the window at the northern Ontario bush without really seeing it, Johnny tried to make sense of his morning. The day before, back at the detachment, his buddies had kidded him, saying the population of Yellow Dog, transformed into a mob of howling savages, would overwhelm the visiting officials and halt the march of progress in the far northern reaches of the province. He was a rookie, just arrived from the south with his wife and three-year-old daughter, and had been prepared for some good-natured kidding from his new colleagues to put him at ease as he started his tour of duty. He had laughed along with the others and hadn't believed for a minute that public disorder of that nature would happen — and he had been right.

But who could have imagined that Steve and the others would play God and implicate him? He would never forgive them or himself. *What have we done?* he asked himself, closing his eyes and refusing to look at the others and the babies. *Since when does the rule of law stop at the boundaries of a reserve? Why were these babies seized and hauled away? Were the mothers not nursing them? Wasn't there food on the table? Had anyone checked to see if the babies had been mistreated?*

Johnny would have been even more upset had he known baby scooping had been going on for a long time. As if it was Big Brother in George Orwell's *1984*, the government had decreed that it wasn't enough to haul all the Native kids ages six to sixteen off to residential schools. "Big Brother" had been doing double duty. For more than a decade, the government had been dispatching Children's Aid Society teams — with no training in Aboriginal history or culture — to carry out quick-and-dirty raids on Yellow Dog and reserves like it across Canada. They were supposed to get the permission of chiefs and council members before they acted, but they never did. They preferred to sneak on to reserves, snatch the babies, and get out of town. They had self-imposed quotas of human flesh to fill — like emissaries of the Roman emperors in ancient times come to collect hostages from conquered tribal peoples beyond their borders.

Eventually, Johnny concluded that it was beyond him, a simple RCMP constable, to make sense of what had happened. Logic and fairness didn't come into play when evil was involved. Brooding over ill-treatment of parents and community and the future of the scooped infants would serve no purpose. The babies, when older, wouldn't remember being removed, but the birth mothers would never forget. The birth mothers and their families, and not the babies, would suffer the immediate emotional consequences. The babies would begin their suffering when they were older and learned the truth.

Johnny wondered how the Makwas were feeling at that moment. They were probably surrounded by family and friends offering comfort. His heart went out to them. He didn't like the way they had stared at him when Hilda and Louise had grabbed their kids. As if it was his fault they were living through the nightmare. Everyone always blamed the cops when they were only following orders. One thing he knew for certain — he wouldn't have stood by if strangers had appeared on his doorstep to take away his daughter! He would have fought them to the death. Maybe Indians didn't love their children as much as white people loved theirs. But perhaps they had been beaten down so much that they had lost their will to resist. Yes, that was it. They had been beaten down.

2

VISIONS OF APOCALYPSE

Had Johnny listened carefully during the van ride back to the plane, he would have heard the heartbreaking death chants and dirges of the Yellow Dog elders from their open windows. They were grieving the loss of the children abducted that day. But they were also venting their helplessness at the ongoing onslaught of the outside world on their way of life, and their anger at yet another arbitrary exercise of power by the Canadian state. How could three hundred people — men, women, children, old people, toddlers, and the infirm included — ever confront the power of the Canadian government backed up that morning by an armed presence of the mighty RCMP? They would have been arrested for hindering the work of the police or some other trumped-up cause and thrown into jail to rot.

From their perspective, the raid was part of a master plan devised by the whites after Confederation in 1867 to do away once and for all with the Indigenous peoples of Canada through assimilation. And of all the heartless measures taken to accomplish this goal, the nastiest was the ongoing attack on children, removing them from their homes on the reserves across the country to send them to residential schools to forget their languages and families. But that had led to the shattering of the family structures of Indigenous peoples as generation after generation of half-educated, broken youth returned to their homes, all too often to neglect and brutalize their own children as they had been neglected and brutalized at the schools. And citing the neglect it had caused as an excuse, the government sent provincial child-welfare officials to take even more children away — but this time to destroy their links with their families and communities by adopting them out.

And what about Indian agent Steve Caruthers? What did he think about baby scooping? If pressed, he would have said something like the following.

First, there were no rallies about baby scooping to join when he was a student at university — and that wasn't his fault. He had been a long-haired, pot-smoking, free-love-supporting university student in the early 1960s who spent his time listening to the protest songs of Bob Dylan and Joan Baez and participating in demonstrations against the Vietnam War and the oppression of blacks in the American South. No one cared about Indians, much less about their babies. Except maybe for their mothers.

Second, he agreed with the practice of baby scooping. Hunters culled deer to improve the stock when their populations became unmanageable, didn't they? Farmers culled their cattle to improve the quality of their herds, didn't they? Removing Indian babies from their parents and giving them to whites who would raise them as whites would diminish the number of Indians and improve Canada's gene pool, wouldn't it?

Third, based on the reports he regularly received from his snitches, and what he imagined went on behind closed doors, he accepted the argument that Indian parents, in contrast to white ones, were inherently incapable of loving their children, and they either abused them or let them run loose throughout their reserves like wild animals escaped from a zoo.

Fourth, like many people, he practised selective compassion and had choices to make. Poverty, food security, infant mortality, female genital mutilation, illiteracy, pest control, clean water, sanitation, shelter, and medical care were his Third World development causes. He picked the struggle against apartheid, the American embargo on trade with Cuba, and the establishment of an independent state of Palestine as his international political priorities. At home in Canada he supported the feminist movement, the fight against ageism, abortion rights, the freedom to smoke pot, and environmentalism. He had no room in his heart to agonize over Indians and their babies. And neither did the government.

Fifth, like most of his buddies back home, he believed Indians had never been and never would be part of his Canada. They were Third World people living in slum-like reserves on the fringes of towns and somewhere up north who just happened to live within the geographical confines of Canada and should be grateful for whatever handouts the government deigned to toss their way.

Sixth, Steve had become so used to treating Indians as wards of the Crown that he had come to believe they were inherently childlike beings, perhaps akin to Neanderthals. It was therefore pointless for governments to provide them with good schools, clean water, and decent housing.

Seventh, Steve was convinced that the best way for society to deal with this strange people's suffering in its midst was to normalize inequity.

The Australians, Steve knew, had once thought they had found the solution to dealing with their First Peoples: separate all half-caste, as they called mixed-blood children, from their Aborigine

mothers as soon as possible after birth, never let them see their birth
mothers again, and raise them in special institutions to become the
servants of whites. The half-castes in the normal course of events
would marry only among themselves or with whites, their children
would follow suit, full-blooded Aborigines would disappear into
the mists of time, all the dreaded inferior Aborigine blood would
be bred out of the Australian gene pool, white Australia would be
preserved, and costs to taxpayers would be slashed.

What could go wrong? Everything, as Steve was aware. Sixty
years of the forced assimilation of what had become known in
Australia as the "Stolen Generations" turned out to be a great flop.
But Canada, Steve also knew, had had its share of flops. Canada's
revered Father of Confederation, Sir John A. Macdonald, tried
starvation as a remedy. Nobody complained about the ethics
of the matter — after all, Indians were subhuman — but given
the scale of the problem, it just wasn't the efficient thing to do.
That sort of barbarism would have to wait for the arrival of Adolf
Hitler years later. Macdonald then switched to removing Indian
kids holus-bolus from their families and imprisoning them for a
decade or more in so-called residential schools "to kill the Indian
in the child," as he put it — even if too often the child was
killed along with the Indian. Canadians from all walks of life
were in favour: Indian agents; politicians of every political stripe;
civil servants; low-class, middle-class, and upper-class Canadians;
professors, schoolteachers, priests, nuns, preachers, and Sunday
school teachers; and editorial writers and other opinion formers.
They all thought it was a brilliant policy but preferred not to
know the details in case their sleep would be disturbed.

That evening, alone in his staff quarters except for the flick-
ering light of his satellite television, Steve reflected on the events of
the day. He felt a deep sense of satisfaction for his role in the operation. His actions to some might have seemed cruel, but someone

had to do this kind of work and he was proud to serve his country in this manner. Babies removed that day would grow up, completely assimilated into mainstream society, not knowing they were Indians and the victims of an ethnic cleansing operation.

After a quiet dinner and a couple of hours watching game shows on television at his government-issue bungalow, Steve went to bed but was bothered by an image that had unexpectedly come to him. The year was 1942, and Yellow Dog Indian Reserve had become a ghetto somewhere in Central Europe with its inhabitants transformed into Jews. He fell asleep listening to the sounds of wolves howling in the bush outside the boundaries of the reserve and dreaming of Nazi soldiers. He woke up the next morning with the conclusion of his dream fresh in his memory: death squads led by a grim-faced nurse, a bewildered child-welfare worker, and a baby-faced RCMP constable had pushed their way into the ghetto, scooped up the children, and taken them away.

3

THE McGREGORS

The float plane with its haul of four baby boys and one baby girl flew uneventfully to Sioux Lookout's airport. Johnny was the first to disembark, anxious to get into his car, return to his detachment, and lose himself in the routine of family life. Like a soldier who did things in wartime only to be ashamed of them later, he would never speak to anyone about the morning's events, nor would he ever again accept similar assignments. Nurse Hilda White and child-welfare worker Louise Bacon carried the bassinets into the passenger lounge, removed the babies one by one, fed them formula, changed their diapers, and did their best to stop their crying. Later they caught an Air Canada flight and were in Toronto in three hours.

Hilda would be killed in a plane crash in the mid-1970s. It also took the lives of a pilot, a child-welfare worker, and an RCMP constable along with a half-dozen scooped babies. Louise took early retirement and opened a bed-and-breakfast but hurriedly got up and left the room whenever anyone mentioned Indigenous people. Afraid of being alone in old age, just before he retired, Steve would marry an Indigenous woman whom he had been seeing quietly for years. They would spend their summers on a lake in northern Ontario close to her family and move to a Florida trailer park for their winters.

All five babies were spoken for. When he was eight months old, one boy went to a family in Texas. His family had paid a for-profit adoption agency in Houston a $15,000 fee to process their application. He was never heard from again. Another boy, adopted by a couple in Markham, Ontario, began showing signs of fetal alcohol syndrome at the age of four. By the age of sixteen, he left home to live on the streets and died of a drug overdose on East Hastings Street, Vancouver's Skid Row. The third boy, one of the Makwa twins, was named Josh and delivered into foster care in a home in northern Winnipeg. He would go from foster home to foster home throughout his childhood and youth until he ended up living on the street.

The fourth boy was adopted by a French-Canadian family in Welland, Ontario. The family were interested in him and not in the colour of his skin, nor who he had been, nor where he had come from. He grew up closely attached to his adoptive parents and siblings and they to him. When he was old enough to understand, his adoptive parents told him he was adopted and offered to help him find his biological parents and learn about his Native heritage. He said he wasn't interested, and he really wasn't. It turned out he would never be a scholar but that didn't matter. His dream was to become a carpenter like his adoptive dad, a wish his dad reciprocated. The fifth child, the other Makwa twin, would be named Brenda and was raised by Nelson and Jean McGregor in the central Ontario town of Orillia.

The McGregors were childhood sweethearts who grew up in the Muskoka village of Campbell's Corners in the heart of one of the most beautiful tourist areas in the country. They loved their community with the same passion as they loved each other. They loved their little no-frills-four-room school with its four rooms, four teachers, and one hundred students attending classes from Grades 1 to 12; their three churches filled with worshippers every Sunday morning; their hockey team that preferred winning fights on the ice to winning games; their service clubs that delivered food packages to the less fortunate; their outstanding library open six days every week; the shops that sold cashmere sweaters and golf jackets to well-heeled summer residents; and the antique steamboats that took tourists on sightseeing excursions on the nearby lakes in the summers.

Nelson and Jean began going steady in Grade 3, were insepar-able from Grades 4 to 12, were married at nineteen in the United Church within two years of graduation, and spent their week-long honeymoon on the Midway at the Canadian National Exhibition in Toronto. They never considered leaving the village to attend college or university. Instead, Jean became the village librarian and Nelson became a plumber. Their happiness would have been com-plete had they been able to have children. But after ten years of trying, visits to the doctor, recourse to old wives' remedies, and the like, they gave up and decided to adopt one of the Indian babies advertised in the Toronto papers who were being removed for their own good by Children's Aid from their northern Ontario families. They placed an order, and within a year, they welcomed Brenda into their family. They loved her so much that they wrote away for another baby and adopted Tammy, another cute little girl from China who was the same age as Brenda. Everybody got along just fine in the enlarged family.

But at that time the McGregors didn't know that when their grandparents had arrived in Muskoka from Northern Ireland in the late nineteenth century they had seen that the best place to settle was already occupied by a community of Ojibwa. The Indian men had fought with the British in the War of 1812 and had been rewarded with the site for their services to the King. That meant nothing to the new arrivals; they complained, and the government sent the Indians packing. That was how things were done in the old days. The newcomers turned the Indian cabins into pigpens, built their own more elaborate homes, ploughed the Indian graves into the ground, threw the bones into the river, and erased the memory of the First Peoples from their collective memory.

One day, carrying out some routine filing in the library, Jean came across yellowing newspapers describing the eviction of the Indians as it had happened in the 1870s. She disclosed this information to Nelson, and they immediately thought of Brenda. They, of course, had no doubts about themselves, but what if the current generation of villagers proved to be as racist as their pioneer forefathers? What sort of life would Brenda have growing up in a village with a hidden stain on its history? Taking no chances, they left the village to start a new life running a motel in Orillia, a hundred kilometres to the south on the shore of Lake Couchiching.

The McGregors pulled both children aside when they were old enough to tell them they had been adopted, saying to Brenda that her parents were Indian, and to Tammy that hers were Chinese. Neither encountered racism at kindergarten or at elementary school. Many of their classmates were the sons and daughters of immigrants from South Asia, and the McGregor girls didn't stand out. They were the top students in their class, and the other kids assumed that was because they both had Chinese birth mothers — and the other children's parents said the Chinese were really smart.

Tammy was everyone's favourite, and that irritated Brenda. Tammy led the class in marks, and Brenda had to content herself with second place. Tammy was always in the school plays, and Brenda was never asked. Tammy was the pretty one, and Brenda was rather plain. Tammy sat with the popular kids in the school cafeteria, and Brenda was left out. Tammy was asked out by boys on dates, and Brenda never was. Brenda thought her parents didn't love her as much as Tammy because she was Indian. And sensing the kids would like her even less if they knew she was Indian, Brenda kept her origins to herself.

When she started high school, a dozen Chippewa students from a nearby reserve joined her Grade 9 homeroom class. They were friendly but didn't believe her when she told them in a whisper that her birth mother was Indian. "Why would someone who's Chinese want to pass as Indian?" they asked. "Or maybe you're an apple Indian — red on the outside and white inside." Thinking she was weird, they avoided her in the hallways and after class.

To Brenda's surprise, she discovered that some of the white kids said nasty things about the Indian kids when they weren't around. Things like "their parents lie around at home all day and live on welfare"; "they smell funny ... must be the raw meat and fish they eat"; "Indians can't ever be trusted"; "Indians leave old mattresses and broken-down wrecks of cars and trucks on their front yards"; "Indians are all drunks"; "Indians sleep on the streets"; "Indians beg to buy beer and neglect their families"; and on and on and on.

Brenda felt terrible at not being accepted by the Indian kids and having to listen to racist stuff from her non-Indian friends about Indian people. That brought to the fore a nagging doubt that there was something wrong with her — a suspicion she had harboured ever since the McGregors had told her that her birth parents were Indian. *Why did they give me away?* she wondered. *What's wrong with me?*

Jean was relieved when Brenda raised her concerns in one of their heart-to-heart talks. "I've been expecting and fearing this conversation for years," she said. "Your birth parents didn't have enough money to provide for all their children and they gave you up when you were only a few months old so someone else could have the joy of welcoming you into their family." When Brenda looked doubtful, Jean continued her make-believe story, saying, "We were the lucky family that got you and have loved you more than if we'd been your birth parents."

"I'd like to meet my real mother," Brenda said. "I'd like to find out if I have brothers and sisters, where they live, whether they're happy, and the things anyone would want to know about their real family."

"But we're your real family now, dear. You might not like what you discover."

In what was likely not a coincidence, the McGregors took their kids to a giant powwow at the SkyDome in Toronto during their last year of high school. There was a reviewing stand in the centre of the playing field framed by standards, flags, and pennants. The air was filled with the smell of sweetgrass and sage. Tens of thousands of people stood in the bleachers. Hundreds of vendors peddled Native crafts, books, and buckskin clothing. Others sold traditional Indigenous foods in kiosks. Representatives of the RCMP, the Canadian Forces, Indian Affairs, the Treasury Board, and the Privy Council worked the crowds, attempting to attract Indigenous recruits to their organizations.

The McGregors hustled their brood to their seats as drummers smashed their batons against dozens of big drums. Elders and war veterans, carrying eagle staffs, moved into position on the walkways and marched in from the eastern entrance, the direction of the rising sun. A thousand dancers wearing eagle-feathered headdresses followed, keeping time to the drumbeats. They swayed, they hopped from foot to foot, they shook their shawls, they rotated slowly in circles, they twisted hoops around their bodies. They advanced slowly and hypnotically in a clockwise direction, like the sun moving across the heavens during the day.

Voices sang out, piercing the rhythmic pounding of the big drums with cries of defiance and screams of pain summoning Brenda to leave her parents and Tammy and join the crowd pouring out of the bleachers to join the stream of dancers. Brenda shuffled forward, her eyes closed, her feet close to the floor, absorbing the energy of the crowd and lamenting and praying along with the others. The people around her, she imagined, were her blood relatives, her birth parents, and she had met them and been accepted and they had told her they loved her, there had been nothing wrong with her, they wanted her back, and she was glad.

But then Brenda felt someone pull her arm and say, "We've got a long way to go, Brenda. You have school tomorrow, you have homework to do, you have chores to do. Snap out of it, Brenda."

She opened her eyes. The music had stopped, the dancers were leaving, and Jean was shaking her and telling her it was time to go.

The next day in school Brenda told the kids in her homeroom class that she was Indian, a Canadian Indian, and not Chinese or an Indian whose roots were in India. But the Chippewa kids laughed at her, and the non-Indian kids applied the venom hitherto reserved for the Chippewa kids to her. Brenda swore that if she ever met her real mother, she would ask why she was given away to strangers. And when Jean and Nelson sent Tammy off to university to study medicine and told Brenda they didn't have the money to do the same for her and to get a job, Brenda left home for good.

PART 2

GREG
1972–1990

4

THE CALVIN MINE

In the summer of 1990, Greg Chambers was an eighteen-year-old with an outstanding academic and sports record who lived with his family in a suburb outside Barrie, Ontario. His parents had worked their way up from blue-collar backgrounds into the ranks of the middle class. His mother, Marg, had served in progressively senior teaching and administrative positions and earned a master of education through part-time courses at the University of Toronto, eventually becoming principal of a major downtown Barrie elementary school. Larry, his father, hadn't reached the professional heights of Marg but nevertheless had been promoted to detective after ten years of service as an Ontario Provincial Police constable. Ten years later he was appointed to the elite Emergency Response Team in charge of dealing with hostage-taking incidents. His buddies looked to him for leadership when they were sent in to save the lives of wives being threatened by their drunken or deranged husbands holed up in their homes around the province. Perhaps that was why they covered for him when he beat up

prisoners when making arrests. The Chambers family gave every
appearance of being a happy one, but that wasn't the case.

Larry and Marg came from big families, and both of them
wanted the same after they married — three or four kids minimum.
It was one of the reasons they had been attracted to each other.
They couldn't have been more delighted when Greg came along
two years after the wedding. Naturally, Marg and Larry thought he
would be followed by a second, and then a third, and who knew,
maybe even a fourth. Having children, they often said to their
friends at church, gave purpose to marriage — gifts from God
sanctifying a holy institution. Imagine their feelings when Marg's
gynecologist told her right after Greg's birth that she wouldn't be
able to have any more children.

Marg was devastated and so was Larry. They had so wanted a
big family. Their distress went beyond disappointment to one of
grief. It was as if they were mourning children yet unborn. Greg's
presence was a constant reminder of the absence of brothers and
sisters and took the bloom off the joy they should have experienced raising him. But then their church pastor, to whom they had
confided their sorrow, told them that if they really wanted an addition to their family, they should consider adopting a Native child,
or even two or three brothers and sisters from the same family unit.
The Children's Aid Society was practically giving them away, no
questions asked. The Ontario government, like the governments
of all other provinces, he said, had been encouraged by the federal
government to seize and adopt out Native children running loose
without proper parental supervision on Indian reserves. But so
many had been taken from their homes that they now constituted
a glut on the market. Some were even being shipped to adoption
agencies across the United States for processing. Such an opportunity to get a healthy Indian child might not happen again. So,
he told them, they should act right away before the offer expired.

Larry, who was an optimist and somewhat naive, tended to believe all the positive stereotypical gibberish he heard about Native people such as being instinctively in tune with nature, never getting lost in the bush, and being innately talented fishermen. He wanted to move quickly to find a little Indian sister for Greg. Marg, on the other hand, didn't believe everything people told her. Her impressions of Natives were obtained from seeing homeless Indians sleeping and begging on the streets of downtown Toronto. Larry reluctantly accepted Marg's suggestion not to proceed and kept to himself his view that she was probably right.

For the first sixteen years of Greg's life, the family spent two weeks each summer canoeing and camping together on a remote lake in Algonquin Park. Each morning, for as long as he could remember, Greg would get up before dawn and fish for pickerel with his dad for two or three hours before heading back to their campsite to prepare a shore breakfast. Larry always took charge, pulling out his razor-sharp knife, gutting and filleting the fish, and tossing the guts to the seagulls circling overhead. "It's time you got the fire going," he would say to his son, who would hurry to place strips of birchbark, cedar kindling, and sticks of wood from dead trees in the firepit, then step back while his dad lit the fire. If the wood caught and a nice fire ensued, Larry would smile and carry on, placing the fillets along with sliced boiled potatoes and onions in a buttered frying pan over the fire to cook as well as a pot of coffee to percolate.

But if the sputtering kindling didn't burst into flames, Larry would scowl, lose his temper, and say any Indian kid half Greg's age could light a fire better, call him a useless tit, and hit him on the side of the head with an open hand. The same thing happened when Greg upset the canoe, and again when a bass he was reeling in leaped high out of the water, spit out the hook, and got away.

The blows were painful, but Greg never cried; he just tried to do a better job the next time. He knew that if Larry didn't wallop him for failures such as these, he could count on the man to lose his temper sooner or later and make him suffer even more for some supposed failing. Despite the ill-treatment, Greg loved the camping trips in Algonquin Park, and Larry would brag for the rest of the year to anyone who would listen about the importance of this annual event as a way of getting close to his son. What Marg thought about being excluded from this male bonding exercise she never said.

Larry slapped Greg around at home, as well, whenever his son irritated him, but he eventually gave up comparing him to the Indian kid that existed only in his imagination. Greg, for his part, would never forget the competition he had faced in his childhood from the non-existent family member. In general, Greg believed his dad was a good dad, taking him to hockey practice and driving him to games, standing up in the bleachers and shouting and swearing at the referees whenever they gave him a penalty, deserved or not. After drinking a half-dozen beers watching football, baseball, or hockey on television in the recreation room on Saturday and Sunday afternoons, Larry would tear up, hug his son, and tell him he loved him. He would say he disciplined him for good reason — his own father had thrashed him regularly when he was a boy and look how he had turned out.

Greg accepted his father's line of reasoning and blows until the spring he turned sixteen. By that time, taking after his mother, who was heavily built and towered over her short and wiry husband, he had grown into a 180-pound, muscled player on the Barrie midget hockey team. When his father sought as usual to physically discipline Greg for some matter of no great consequence, Greg snapped and fought back, punching him in the face and knocking him to his knees. As Larry got to his feet, his eyes registered surprise rather than anger.

"Hit me again, you bastard," Greg snarled, "and you'll get more of the same."

Greg's father hadn't been hurt. In fact, he laughed, seemingly proud of the spunk shown by his son, but from that moment the summer canoe trips ended and he never struck Greg again. Instead, whenever his son did something that upset him, he took out his anger on his wife, punching her in the stomach, breast, and ribs and yanking her hair. As a cop who carefully avoided leaving marks on the faces of the prisoners he beat up to avoid awkward questions from his sergeant, he knew enough never to blacken his wife's eyes or cut her face with his blows. Marg was grateful for her husband's thoughtfulness and never fought back or complained to the cops. What could she do about it, anyway? Larry had been beating her for years, ever since they were married, actually. She was sure of his love and had always taken it.

Marg had reasons for her fortitude. Above all, she loved the guy and wouldn't do anything to disappoint him. She also had a reputation as a respected educator to maintain and certainly didn't want the neighbours to know. It would have been a calamity if her husband was fired. It would have been awful if he was expelled from the Lions Club. It would have been embarrassing to face the knowing stares from her friends among the wives of her husband's OPP colleagues. Besides, in the greater scheme of things, to get a thumping now and then wasn't such a big deal. When she was growing up, her own father, when he drank, had beaten her mother, and they'd had a happy marriage, or so she assumed. Lots of men in those days beat their wives, and it hadn't been the end of the world. She was sure it was still going on.

From his dad, Greg inherited a streak of ruthlessness and misogyny, and from his mother, a love of classical music and good books. He was a worrier with a touch of cold calculation that was off-putting to his friends. Intellectually, he was somewhat of a prodigy and always at the head of his school class. He spent much of his free time at the Barrie public library borrowing books on the big international issues of the day such as the introduction of perestroika and glasnost in the Soviet Union, the tearing down of the Berlin Wall, the freeing of the Central European satellite countries, the anti-apartheid struggle in South Africa, and the intifada on the West Bank and in Gaza. But he was either blind to the big social issues simmering in Canada such as gay marriage, systemic discrimination against Aboriginal people, climate change, and women's rights, or more likely, didn't care about them.

In his opinion, only one among the 150 government leaders on the planet deserved to be called great — that was his hero, Fidel Castro. Nelson Mandela came a close second, but he had been locked away for years. Whenever a new biography of the Cuban leader's life came out, Greg dipped into his savings to buy it. He never tired of reading about Castro's attack on the Moncada barracks in Santiago, Cuba, that launched the revolution, his long guerrilla warfare against the Batista regime from his mountain hideout, his triumphal march into Havana on New Year's Eve 1959, the defeat inflicted on a CIA-supported invasion force in 1961, and so much more, such as sending troops to fight the white South Africans in Angola and fomenting revolution in Central America. It was Greg's dream to travel to Cuba one day and shake the hand of the maximum leader. He dreamed about making a mark on the world as great as that made by Castro, but in the world of ideas.

Greg spent his free time thinking about big questions such as What was the meaning of life? Where did the world come from? Why was there something rather than nothing? Was there such a thing as nothing? Did anything exist before the Big Bang? Could special relativity and quantum gravity be reconciled? What was eternity? Did God exist? What happened after death? Why was there suffering in the world? How did one make moral choices? And other issues of a similar nature. Greg took a liking to great writers who were philosophers, especially Friedrich Nietzsche and his nihilism, Titus Lucretius Carus and his arguments against the fear of death, and Fyodor Dostoyevsky and his irrational passion.

He planned out his life well in advance. Greg had been going steady since Grade 7 with a girl named Crystal whom he had met at church, and they talked vaguely of getting married someday. She said she wanted three or four kids, and he said that was fine with him. She said she wanted a house in the suburbs and a summer cottage on Lake Simcoe, and he had no objection. They mentioned their plans to their parents, who agreed with them. Greg's career goal was to become a trade commissioner in the Department of Foreign Affairs and International Trade, known to insiders as the "Department," and become in due course a deputy minister. Crystal agreed.

On graduation from high school at age eighteen, Greg was admitted to Carleton University and enrolled in its four-year International Affairs Program. As a responsible son, he had no desire to burden his parents with his tuition fees, accommodation, and other expenses. He found a well-paying summer job working as a kitchen helper two hundred kilometres north of the town of Murdoch in northeastern Manitoba.

Early one morning in mid-June 1990, still believing he would fulfill his destiny and do great things in life, Greg said goodbye to his mother and joined his father waiting in the family car to drive him to the Greyhound bus station. As Larry put the car into gear and headed into town, Greg heard his father say as if from far away,

"You'll see. It won't be so hard up there. You'll get a cozy job in the kitchen far from the mineshaft. You'll make friends. There'll probably be good fishing. We'll be thinking of you. Call us if you get homesick. Before you know it, you'll be home eating your mother's cooking and watching a football game on television with me. We might even have a beer or two before you set off for university."

Greg scarcely paid any attention to his father's ramblings. Already homesick, he was now in another world, staring out the window and bidding farewell to the city of his childhood and youth as he began another phase in his life. At the bus station Larry waited until Greg bought a ticket, walked with him to the bus, shook hands with him stiffly, gave him a hug, and wiped tears from his eyes. Greg didn't look or wave from the window when the bus pulled away.

Two days later he arrived at his destination deep in the black-spruce boreal bush, getting off in the late morning at the local coffee shop that also served as the bus station. While he was still pulling his suitcase from the pile of luggage beside the bus, he heard someone say, "I suppose you're Greg Chambers, the summer student. You guys stick out like sore thumbs."

After Greg acknowledged that he was indeed the summer student, a short, fat, bearded man, a caricature of a lumberjack with plaid shirt tucked in over his paunch, braces holding up his pants, and a baseball cap emblazoned with the emblem of the Montreal Expos, introduced himself as Hubert Leduc, sent to drive him to his new place of work.

"The van's over there," Hubert said, leading the way to his vehicle. "Climb aboard and let's get going. We've got a ways to go before we get to the Calvin — that's what everyone calls the mine."

Hubert talked non-stop for the next four hours. "I'm Métis," he told Greg. "A proud Métis, not like those guys who are ashamed of having a little Indian blood in their veins and pretend to be

French. My family's lived around here for generations before Louis Riel was even thought of — hunting, trapping, and fishing, trading for furs with the Indians, anything to make a buck. Now what about you? Where are you from? Where'd your people come from? Are you from around here? You a Métis? You could pass for one with your black hair and high cheekbones. Maybe we're long-lost cousins. Wouldn't that be something! What do you say? What are they giving you to do at the Calvin?"

"When did they put in this gravel road?" Greg asked, changing the subject.

"Well, now, that's a long story. There's three Indian reserves making up the Amalgamated Wawatay Cree Tribal Council strung out along the road up there in the bush, and an Indian residential school on a godforsaken lake some distance away from the Calvin where they fly the kids from around the north in and out. In the old days, they used dog teams in the winters and canoes in the summers to get around. The chiefs agitated for years for the government to put in an all-weather road so they could get out whenever they wanted to buy supplies in the stores at Murdoch and take sick people to doctors and hospitals, but the government did nothing. And then about thirty years ago someone found gold on their traditional lands and everything changed. Suddenly, the government began the road and crews started work on the Calvin."

"How did everything turn out?" Greg asked.

"It's been a success, I guess. It took a few years for the road and mine to be finished. Now the mine employs about two hundred people who work on-site. Good wages and working conditions, staff quarters for everybody, gym, lounge, satellite TV, top-of-the-line grub, eight days of holidays for every fourteen worked. Except for you students who are stuck there all summer. Everyone's happy except the Indians. None of them got jobs."

"Not that it's any of my business, but why's that?"

"Don't be stupid, kid. Here's the deal. On paper they were supposed to get jobs, the Calvin being on their lands. But management always rigs the written tests so the Indians, who can barely read and write, fail."

After a short silence to allow Greg to think about his words, Hubert continued. "I used to live hand-to-mouth just like an Indian around here before I got steady work and good wages at the Calvin. Now I sweep and wash floors at the staff complex and do these runs to Murdoch." After glancing with a tight smile at his passenger, Hubert added, "But if you get bored, there's always the Zoo for entertainment up there. That's a cedar-log tavern some guys opened up a few years ago. It's on no man's land just outside the Calvin property line and close but not on a reserve.

"Why's it called the Zoo?

"Its real name is Northern Delights Bar and Grill, but everyone calls it the Zoo. And that's because the people who go there behave like animals — fighting, shouting, laughing, crying, breaking beer bottles, singing along with the cowboy music, screwing, and hell knows what else. And not just the Indians. White people get into the spirit, too. The management lets in bikers and underage guys, kids from the residential school, anyone at all, and they can drink and make fools of themselves as much as they want as long as their money lasts. It's said someone even brought a bear and let it go inside just for the hell of it. Guys drive all the way from Murdoch to get a piece of ass, get drunk, and let it all hang loose."

"Why do the cops let them get away with it?"

"It's a safety valve, kid. The powers that be around here are glad the Zoo's there. It's a place where a lot of steam is let off by a lot of people on weekends, leaving them too worn out to cause trouble the rest of the week. Mine management would rather its crews drink and trash the Zoo instead of the staff complex. Maybe that's why the cops sit outside in the parking lot and never go in, even when there's been a murder or there's a riot going on."

After a short silence to prepare his message, Hubert came to the point he had wanted to make from the start. Catching Greg's eye, he lowered his voice and said, "Just between you and me, kid, I run a little bootlegging business. Nothing special, but if you ever get thirsty, come see me and I'll fix you up. If you want a girl, an Indian girl, I mean — there's no available white women where we're going — I can arrange that, as well. I sometimes take guys, women, and a case or two of beer on a dirt track that runs through the bush behind the Zoo to the Desolation River where absolute privacy is guaranteed."

"What's the history behind that river's name?" Greg asked.

"I've heard it was called that after some crazy explorer nearly starved to death trying to map it a hundred years ago. It's shallow, rocky, unforgiving, and goes nowhere — nobody and nothing around for kilometres. Lucky for the explorer, the Indians rescued him."

Greg asked no further questions for the rest of the trip.

"C'mon, kid, lighten up and have a little fun." Hubert had tracked down Greg that evening in the staff complex. "The Indians have just got their welfare cheques and are blowing their money at the Zoo, getting falling-down drunk and fighting and generally making fools of themselves."

"Doesn't sound like fun to me," Greg said, hoping Hubert would go away.

"But I wanna celebrate your arrival by showing you a good time. It's better than reality TV. There's nothing going on around here, anyway. Let's go and have some laughs. And if you want, I'll line you up with a sweet Indian girl from the residential school and maybe you'll get lucky."

Greg would later tell himself he accepted only because he didn't believe Hubert. That people would drink and drink until they lost control of themselves and start fighting among themselves was too foreign an idea to be credible — at least to someone who had led a sheltered life. So why not go and have a draft beer or two? After all, he was eighteen and had never been inside a bar. Might even be good training for university life in the fall. If, in fact, Hubert was right and the place was as bad as he said, all the better. It was time he saw how the other half lived.

"I knew you'd come," Hubert said after Greg told him he'd go but only for one or two beers. "Nobody's gonna pour beer down your throat or force you to stay. You just say the word and we'll leave."

Hubert hadn't been exaggerating about the Zoo. An unsmiling bouncer opened a steel-clad door and motioned Hubert and Greg inside. A giant television screen fixed high on a wall showed a baseball game that no one was watching. From Greg's vantage point at the top of the stairs, the room below looked like a pit of writhing snakes, but instead of snakes, bikers in leather jackets, truckers in shirtsleeves, and mine employees with the logo of their employer on their sweatshirts, together with Indian men and women, were on the move, weaving around tables, sitting down, standing up, shouting out greetings, waving to friends, slapping backs, and screaming hysterically in a cacophonic jumble of voices. The intoxicating smell of raw sex, testosterone, cigarette smoke, and beer filled the room. Thunderous and indecipherable country-and-western music poured out of giant speakers. White men laughed at Indians who laughed right back at them, as if the two sides were engaged in a sort of bizarre laughing contest. It could have been a Hieronymus Bosch painting of a world in which sinners were reliving their lives in a hell of eternal laughter.

Hubert nudged Greg to get his attention and led him to a table with two empty places. A T-shirt-wearing waiter, naked women tattooed on his biceps, came by, dumped a beer-drenched tray on the table, and slid a gallon pitcher of beer and two glasses toward them. Greg pulled out his wallet to pay, but Hubert pushed his hand away and said, "Your money's no good here. Tonight you're my guest. And now let me show you how I do it." He downed the contents of his glass in one swallow.

"And this is how I do it," Greg said, raising his glass to do the same. But he choked and spit beer out onto the table, causing Hubert to laugh. "That was my first beer, but it won't be my last." Greg filled his glass again and downed the second beer in a single gulp.

"I bet you've never been laid, either," Hubert said. When Greg didn't answer, he added, "I thought so. But I'll fix that tonight."

5

IN THE WRONG PLACE

Too many beers on top of two days of continuous travel on the Greyhound with only a few snatches of sleep rendered Greg semi-comatose. He was vaguely aware of Hubert guiding him as he stumbled out the door of the Zoo. Sometime later he came to in the front seat of the van to hear Hubert in the back raping a moaning woman and shouting. "Hold still or I'll kick the shit out of you." After falling asleep again, he opened his eyes in the predawn light of the northern bush to see Hubert rhythmically whacking something lying on the ground outside with a tire iron. "That'll teach you to give me lip! I'll teach you who's boss!"

Hubert tossed the tire iron to one side, glanced at the van, and smiled when he saw Greg staring wide-eyed and unbelieving at the Indian girl — it wasn't a woman, after all — on the ground. "Sometimes they don't co-operate and I gotta dole out some punishment." He grimaced. "I taught her who was boss. I taught her good. Now I need your help to get rid of her."

Greg didn't move.

"You son of a bitch, if you hadn't wanted Indian ass, this wouldn't have happened." Hubert yanked open the front passenger door and pulled him out. "I've a mind to do the same to you. Now take one arm and I'll take the other and we'll dump her in the Desolation. That'll take care of the problem."

Greg did as he was told, not because he didn't want to argue, not because he was afraid of Hubert, but because he was too drunk to think straight. He would later remember helping drag a girl down a cut-over rocky slope, crushing blueberry and blackberry bushes underfoot and soaking his pants in the morning dew. Partway there, the girl became entangled in the brambles, and he gave up, dropped to his knees, and released his hold.

"For Christ's sake, Greg, keep going. We gotta get this done. She may be small, but I can't do this alone. You're in this as much as me."

Greg stumbled to his feet, seized the girl's arm again, and helped Hubert manoeuvre her through a thick growth of blueberry bushes on the side of a gorge carved out of the land by the fast-flowing water below. But just after he helped Hubert swing the still-moaning girl out into the rapids, the fragrance of wild blueberries that he had loved so much during camping trips in Algonquin Park filled the air. He looked up to see the black sky turn light and the sun rise over the black spruces across the river and to hear birds in their thousands along the shore and in the bush burst out in song, hailing the dawn of a new day. And then, just as he was beginning to believe he would never feel so alive again, he was suddenly confused. *Where am I? What am I doing? Did I just help a stranger throw a girl to her death into a river somewhere in northern Manitoba?*

Then he heard Hubert say, "Let's get out of here. Never know when someone might come along. Get a move on!"

* * *

The next morning Greg woke up smelling blueberries in his room at the staff complex. He got out of bed, went to the window, and looked out — a beautiful day, white cumulus clouds in a deep blue sky. Greg remembered drinking too much, and good old Hubert taking care of him. He smiled when he recalled downing beer after beer at the Zoo and joking around with the other customers...really going to enjoy working up here...already met one guy to hang out with...held my own with my first beers...smoked my first cigarettes...no need to tell my parents anything — they wouldn't understand. But as he stood at the window staring out, an image of Hubert raping and beating an Indian teenager on the back floor of the van came to him. The scene shifted, and he was watching as Hubert hit the girl, now lying outside on the ground, with a tire iron. He was then helping Hubert drag her through the brush and throw her from a clifftop into a river as the sun rose over the black spruces, with all the birds in creation singing their hearts out in music so beautiful he wanted to cry. The images were so unbelievable that Greg was sure they were memories of nightmares induced by too much booze. *Yes,* he thought, *just nightmares. I'll tell Hubert about it when I see him. He'll have a good laugh.*

But when he reported for work later that morning and came across him having coffee in the cafeteria, Hubert told him to shut up when he began to tell him about his nightmare. "That weren't no bad dream, you stupid son of a bitch," he snapped, keeping his voice low. "Meet me after work and I'll fill you in. In the meantime, keep your trap shut about what happened if you don't want to end up in jail."

Greg was shaken when Hubert told him what had really happened when they met after dinner in a quiet corner of the staff complex lounge. "It's all your fault," Greg said in a low voice. "You did the dirty work, not me. Don't mention me when the cops come knocking on your door. I've got a whole life ahead of me."

"Don't worry, nothing's going to happen," Hubert said, trying to calm him down. "I've been through this before, more than once, in fact, and the cops have never bothered me. No one lives along that river and she's probably ten kilometres downstream by now and moving fast in the white water. The crows, vultures, and eagles will get to her, and before you know it, there'll be nothing left but a few bones for the coyotes and wild dogs to crunch for the marrow. Nobody'll ever be able to identify her. Besides, no one up here gives a damn about Indians."

"You're shitting me," Greg said. "Nobody disappears without a trace like that. She's probably already been reported missing, and her friends and family and the cops are beating the bushes this very minute for her. Soon the military will have a helicopter up searching the river. Divers will be called in. My dad's a cop, and he's been on lots of these hunts for missing people. They almost always find who they're looking for — dead or alive. And if they're dead, they always get the guys that did it and bring them to justice. So don't give me any more of that crap!"

"Take it easy," Hubert said. "I'll walk you through what's going to happen. If, and it's a big if, she was from the residential school, when they do the roll call Monday morning, they'll mark her down as absent, not missing. No one will get excited because it's end-of-term and the teachers will think she's walking home through the bush."

"Wouldn't the parents at least ask questions?"

"No, and I'll tell you why. Residential schools are so disorganized some of them would never get around to telling them their daughter's absent or missing. And if the parents wonder why their kid didn't come home for the summer, they'd say, 'Oops, forgot to mention it, but she ran away and we thought she'd made it home. Don't blame us. So many kids run away we can't keep track of them. Sorry for your loss.'"

"But if they report her missing instead of absent?"

"For the sake of argument, if they reported her missing and filled out the paperwork, the Mounties would take note of their statement but file it away and do nothing. Students of all ages at that place go missing all the time. They're always running away, trying to make it home to their reserves. Some never make it because they're just little kids, or they didn't have supplies or proper clothing, or because they get lost in the bush, or because a bear decides to eat them and that's the fault of nobody."

"What if it was someone from the reserve and the family went straight to the cops?"

"The Mounties still wouldn't touch it. They never do nothing when there's Indians, especially Indian women, involved. They don't want to drive two hundred kilometres over a dusty gravel road to do an investigation. They don't want to be bothered. They don't like Indians."

"But what if the family got hold of the local member of Parliament to get action?"

"They'd say she probably got drunk and wandered off into the bush and got lost. Maybe hitchhiked south and was now a hooker in Winnipeg. That's what they always say when Indian women disappear, whether it's the truth or not. No reason to believe they'd treat this case any different.

"Wouldn't the parents be frantic with worry?"

"Look, kid, I've spent my life around Indians. I've even got a few relatives who are Indians, and I can't never tell what they're thinking. They won't crack a smile when I say something funny. But when they say something stupid, something not the least bit funny, at least to me, they laugh their heads off. That proves they're not the same as white people like us. They don't feel things like us. Honest to God, they don't think, see, feel, hear, or taste things like us. They don't grieve their dead like us. That means we didn't throw a girl off that cliff. We threw *something* that looked like a girl into the Desolation."

"Does that mean you don't feel sorry for her?"

"Good God, kid, how many times have I got to tell you! Indians aren't like us. They're not real people like us. The white man found them living like animals in the bush when he came here years back in the old days. They lived like animals and thought like animals. In my opinion, they haven't changed that much. That's why the government set up those residential schools. To educate the animal nature out of them. But it hasn't been working. They don't know what's good for them and run away all the time."

"Nobody in their right mind would believe what you just said."

"Now tell me something, kid. Do you feel sorry for that Indian girl?"

"To be honest, Hubert, I feel guilty about what happened, but not really sorry. Indians have never been my favourite people. Maybe it's because it all happened so fast and I was drunk. Maybe it's because I didn't see her face. Maybe it's because she wasn't white and hadn't lived a life like mine. Maybe sorrow will kick in when I've had time to think about it some more."

"You've just proved my point. Nobody would feel sorry for someone who wasn't fully human. White men should save their tears for murdered white girls, not murdered Indian ones."

"What if by some miracle the body's found?"

"I don't believe in miracles. That body will never be found."

"But what if her body's found?"

"I just said that body will never be found."

"That's hard to believe. This is Canada, after all."

"It's not the Canada you're used to. Up here there's no bus service to the south, so the people on the reserves go out on the side of the road and stick out their thumbs. The girls, especially the good-looking ones, have no trouble getting rides. But they gotta pay a price. There's no free lunch. They gotta put out or get out."

"What happens if they don't put out?"

"Then too bad for them. If they're lucky, they're just kicked out of the vehicle in the middle of nowhere. Sometimes they're raped first, especially if there's two or three guys in the car, because those bitches fight like crazy, just like the one we dumped in the Desolation. And when they're dumped in that place, you know what happens. I should know because lots of guys up here get rid of Indian women that way. Up here we call it disappearing them. And before you get preachy, it's not a racist thing. More Indians are killed by their husbands and boyfriends than by white guys like me."

"How do you know?"

"I just know."

"But murder is murder," Greg said. "Race has nothing to do with it."

"You're just a pup. You'll learn. The rules are different up here."

"But the Mounties have this great reputation. I could understand if they took their time dealing with one missing woman. But a whole series of them? That I can't believe."

"Believe it or not, the Mounties up here aren't the nice ones who pose for pictures with tourists on Parliament Hill. They do what they want when it comes to Indians."

"I'm still not convinced," Greg said. "We need to keep our stories straight if they come after us."

"All we need to say is we don't know nothing. We went to the Zoo, had a few drinks, and went home to bed. It'd be our word against that of anyone who wanted to tie us to the case."

Nevertheless, Greg went to bed each night filled with fear and unable to sleep. One evening, lying on his sofa, he began to dream.

He was a boy of ten again, on a warm summer morning away from his bickering parents, fishing from his canoe. A warm breeze out of the south blew away the bugs, and the air was fragrant with the scent of white pine and balsam needles. Canada geese flew overhead, and loons called to one another in a language only they understood. He had never been so alive, never felt so full of joy. A white-tailed deer with a rack of antlers stepped out of the shadows into the shallow water and looked him in the eyes.

Suddenly, his dream changed and he was standing on the shore of the Desolation River downstream from the gorge, watching transfixed as the body of the teenage Indian girl floated toward him. He knew what would happen next and tried to escape. But his legs refused to move, and the girl opened her eyes and asked, "Why you and not me? Why you and not me?" She was telling him that life was a game of chance. He could have been born rich or poor, white or Indian, the son of middle-class parents in a Barrie suburb or the daughter of a poor Cree trapper. Good luck had favoured him until he visited the Zoo when bad luck had come. Bad luck had led Hubert to the Indian teenager. She was telling him that his plans for a comfortable future could change in an instant. All it would take would be a zealous cop to arrest him and a court to send him to jail.

But nothing happened. Greg pawed through the police reports in the Winnipeg newspapers in the lounge of the staff complex. There were the usual stories of murdered and disappeared Indian women, but nothing about a girl gone missing near the Calvin. Hubert was right The rules were different up here. She was just an Indian no one cared about. He'd try to put the incident behind him and stay out of trouble.

Greg continued to worry, though. Maybe Hubert was wrong. Maybe the police up here cared about Indians. Maybe plainclothes detectives had been dispatched to launch an investigation.

Maybe at that very moment they were talking to waiters and patrons at the Zoo. Maybe they were on their way to take him to jail. Maybe police cars would soon be pulling up to the staff complex. Soon they would be knocking on his door and asking him to accompany them to Mountie headquarters in Murdoch. In the lobby, Hubert would be resisting arrest and saying Greg had dragged the half-dead girl all by himself to the gorge overlooking the Desolation River and thrown her still alive down into the rapids to drown and float away.

Greg's moaning kept him awake at nights. He was plagued by nightmares in which he'd done something terrible. Something that would ruin his life. He had killed someone, someone whose face he couldn't see, someone he didn't know, someone who hadn't deserved to die. And worst of all, when the nightmare ended and he woke up, the horror was still there. He was guilty. He was going to be punished. He had committed an unforgivable crime that would ruin his life.

Before the summer ended, Greg walked the three kilometres to the Zoo, taking fright when he saw an RCMP cruiser in the parking lot with two policemen inside watching patrons come and go. *They're not here for me,* he told himself hopefully, then went inside, took a seat in a distant corner, and ordered a beer.

Hubert came over and joined him. "I didn't want to mention it, but you owe me for services rendered. I found you a girl just as I said I would and you owe me a hundred bucks."

"Bugger off," Greg said. "Don't bother me again."

Hubert sat for a few minutes in silence before drifting away to sit with a lone trucker and talk with him earnestly.

He's offering bootlegger and pimp services, Greg thought. *If the guy raises his voice and waves Hubert off, the pitch hasn't worked. But if they put their heads together, talk in whispers, and leave the room together and don't come back, then an Indian girl or woman will be raped and maybe murdered tonight.*

6

THE SEARCH FOR REDEMPTION

Marg and Larry met Greg at the Barrie Greyhound terminal. When they saw his face, they assumed the summer at the mine had made him thoughtful and mature and had been good for him. They had no idea that the son they had said goodbye to in mid-June wasn't the same person who came back. But they knew that all wasn't well when he took to his room and stayed there, except for short breaks for meals, until he left for Ottawa a week later.

On the first day back, Greg narrowed his options to two possibilities. Should he do the right thing, go to the police, confess, and take his punishment like a man? Or should he forget about what had happened and just get on with life? He decided to do the right thing. But then he thought about what that would entail, the punishment, the disgrace, the shame, the end to his brilliant career prospects, and the shock and disappointment of his parents who had such great hopes for him. He thought about life cooped up behind prison bars, reading porn magazines, playing checkers, and fending off horny felons. He thought about his hockey coach and buddies who would begin by not believing he was capable of committing such a crime but end up cursing him for what he had done.

Greg changed his mind and decided to go for option two: to get on with life and hope the police would never catch him. But this superficially easy choice came with costs. He would have to deal with unending uncertainty, afraid every policeman he encountered on the street or passing by in a patrol car was coming to arrest him. Worst of all, he would have to contend with his conscience, a fearsome guardian of his morality with a life of its own nourished by years of Sunday morning church services listening to sermons based on the Beatitudes:

> Blessed are the poor in spirit: for theirs is the kingdom of Heaven.
> Blessed are those who mourn: for they will be comforted.
> Blessed are the meek: for they will inherit the earth.
> Blessed are those who hunger and thirst after righteousness: for they will be fulfilled.
> Blessed are the merciful: for they will be shown mercy.
> Blessed are the pure in heart: for they will see God.
> Blessed are the peacemakers: for they will be called the children of God.
> Blessed are those who are persecuted for righteousness sake: for theirs is the Kingdom of Heaven.
> Blessed are you when others revile you and persecute you and utter all kinds of evil against you falsely on my account. Rejoice and be glad, for your reward in heaven is great, for so they persecuted the prophets who were before you.

But there was nothing poor in spirit, mournful, meek, merciful, righteous, peaceable, and pure in heart about drinking oneself into a stupor and helping murder a defenceless Indian girl — and by not going to the police and taking the punishment he deserved. Greg added another option to give himself some flexibility: find a way to salve his conscience while escaping punishment and getting on with life. Finding a solution, though, wouldn't be easy.

Greg slid the CD of Beethoven's late string quartets into the player and went to bed, hoping inspiration would come to him in the night. The next morning he woke up, thinking he had the answer: not go to prison and get on with life but appease his conscience by becoming a perfect son to his parents, a perfect husband to Crystal, a perfect father to his as yet unborn children, a perfect member of the church he would attend each Sunday, a perfect university student whatever that entailed, and a perfect trade commissioner if he was taken on — in short, he would pay for his wrongdoings by becoming a perfect person. But on second thought, he realized he was incapable of becoming a perfect person. In his heart of hearts, he was a dirty, contaminated, sinful, unforgivable creature fit only to associate in prison with degenerates like himself. But after thrashing around for days for a better alternative, he found a path out of his dilemma: he would dedicate his life with all its imperfections to doing penance by helping Indigenous people.

Greg's behaviour — isolating himself in his room and answering their questions about his summer in noncommittal monosyllables — irritated his parents. To teach him a lesson, Marg didn't offer him a piece of the blueberry pie she had baked expressly for him as a homecoming gift, and Larry didn't invite him to watch a football game on television and drink a beer with him. They also insisted he go to see poor neglected Crystal, who, they claimed, had been waiting beside the telephone for him to call.

So, to discuss their future, Greg asked Crystal to a local pizza parlour. He held her hand in his, looked into her eyes, and told her it was time they went their separate ways. He would be at university for four years to get his undergraduate degree — five or six if he added on a master's program — and would need at least that much time to think about his future. Crystal jumped in to say they should get married right away. He had evidently returned from northern Manitoba troubled about something. They could work through his problems together. She could help put him through university. Greg said no. They were both too young to make commitments. Crystal got the message, and the relationship was over.

Larry and Marg were relieved when the time came for Greg to depart for university. He left on a Saturday morning in a used white camper with tinted windows that his father had purchased as a farewell gift. He brought everything he needed to furnish his new quarters: clothes, a bed, sheets and blankets, dishes, pots and pans, his CD player, his collection of classical music, his favourite books, and an old sofa. Ottawa's ByWard Market, where his apartment was located, was thronged by day with people buying fresh fruits and vegetables and lunching in one of its fashionable cafés. In the evenings, tourists having dinner packed its restaurants. After the customers paid their bills and went back to their rooms to watch the late news, the women of the street came out to service another sort of clientele: lonely men in search of female companionship and on the lookout for sex.

Greg's priority that fall of 1990, apart from his university classes, was to study the Amalgamated Wawatay Cree Tribal Council to learn about the people of the girl he had helped murder. He found that they were Woodland Cree who had moved hundreds of years before from their ancestral home in the Hudson Bay lowlands to higher ground in the interior where game was more abundant. The Dominion of Canada came into being, the control of Indians passed from Britain to Canada, the *Indian Act* came into force, and the people were herded like animals onto small reserves. Their children were then taken from them and sent to residential schools, and outsiders ignorant of Indian culture and languages seized thousands of a new generation of babies in the Sixties Scoop to be raised as whites. When those mistaken initiatives failed, the government walked away, leaving Indigenous family structures in ruins. Indian husbands, crazed by the depths to which their people had fallen, beat and killed their wives, while the dregs of white male society preyed on the Indian girls and women left standing.

Broadening his search throughout the four years of his undergraduate studies, Greg paid attention to how the issue of murdered and missing Indigenous women was covered in the media. He noted that Betty Osborne, a nineteen-year-old high school girl from Norway House Indian Reserve near The Pas, Manitoba, had been murdered by four white men but that one and only one of the assailants had been convicted. He followed a sickening scandal in British Columbia involving police incompetence in dealing with the disappearance of dozens of women from Vancouver's Downtown Eastside. And hundreds of Indigenous women and girls were being murdered or going missing, just like the girl he had helped throw into the Desolation River — but the stories were on the back pages of the newspapers. The press didn't seem to care.

Greg's search for understanding became an obsession. He visited Friendship Centres, attended powwows, and took part in sit-ins on Parliament Hill. He met Indigenous people by the dozen; shared meals of wild rice, bannock, and moose meat; and listened for hours to their views on how to improve the living conditions of their people. But despite his best efforts, his conscience continued to remind him that he really should have turned himself in to the law and pay the price for murder.

Then, late one night, he was driving back to his apartment in his camper van when he spotted an Indigenous sex worker standing in a doorway. Pulling over, he leaned out the window. She walked over and began listing the types of services she offered. Greg turned on his charm and said he just wanted to talk. She thought he must be crazy, might hurt her, and started to walk away. Greg called out to say he lived in the neighbourhood and wanted to hang out. Since business was slow and Greg seemed like a clean-cut young man, she took him up on his offer to buy her a cup of coffee at an all-night restaurant. They talked about the Academy Awards, who was sleeping with whom in Hollywood, the weather, and the other banal subjects that people discuss when they have nothing better to do.

The next night he sought her out, and she introduced him to some friends. In the coming weeks, they told him their stories of beatings by husbands and boyfriends, childhoods spent being sexually assaulted, grinding poverty, endemic racism, harassing cops, suicidal children, and alcoholism and drug addiction.

He felt their pain. They were people, just as he was a person. He felt sorry for them and for the Indian girl he'd helped murder and for suffering Aboriginals everywhere. The sex workers became friends. He felt compassion for their lot in life. He felt a shared humanity for Indigenous people everywhere. It was then but a short step to wanting to become an Indigenous person himself. The problem was he didn't have a drop of Indigenous blood in his veins. No matter. He convinced himself that every man, woman, and child on the planet was Indigenous. To skeptics, he would say science was on his side. He would patiently explain that just before the moment of the Big Bang everything and everyone — the stars, planets, black holes, dark matter, time, space, dinosaurs, warm-

and cold-blooded animals, fish, and white, brown, yellow, and red persons, and all the colours in between — were bound together in potentiality. And after the Big Bang, everything and everyone shared the same atoms. Or so he thought. He wasn't completely sure. He wasn't an astrophysicist.

But Greg was certain that if you went back just a couple of million years or so, around the time Lucy was supposed to have led her friends out of Africa, you would discover that everybody was related to everyone — Africans to Europeans to Asians to Indigenous people — and taken together, that made the Indigenous people white and the white people Indigenous. He could also say that a heritage organization had lent credence to his theory by announcing it had discovered that fully 25 percent of the citizens of the United States had a few Native American genes in their genomes. Since Canada was just across the border from the United States, it stood to reason that the same thing applied to Canadians, as well. If it applied to Canadians, it applied to Greg.

And if all this science or pseudo-science wasn't enough, Greg convinced himself that all you had to do was tell yourself that feeling Indigenous trumped blood quantum levels and make your choice: Indian, Métis, or Inuit. Greg considered his options and decided to be Métis. He wore his hair pulled back, dyed black, and twisted into one big braid. He coloured his skin light brown and was never seen without a buckskin jacket with fringes. Allowing himself a little lie, he said that a great-great-great-grandmother on his father's side of the family had been a Georgian Bay Métis and that made him Métis. He let it be known among his circle of acquaintances that he was Métis, and since they were used to people telling the truth, they believed him. And if that wasn't enough, to complete his transformation he wore a red sash, ate tourtière, listened to fiddle music, and danced the jig on Louis Riel's birthday.

PART 3

BRENDA AND GREG
1995–1996

7

THE DATING SITE

In November 1995, twenty-three years after the baby scoopers raided the Yellow Dog Indian Reserve, Brenda McGregor was living in Ottawa in an apartment she shared with three colleagues from work. After graduating with honours in Native studies from the University of Ottawa, she had landed a well-paying position as a program officer at Indian Affairs and had grown into a serene, almost cheerful young woman who made friends easily. But her background as an adopted-out fully assimilated child and adolescent raised in a white middle-class environment had left its mark. No matter how many Indigenous friends she made, no matter how many powwows and demonstrations she attended, she still harboured doubts about her identity as an Indigenous person. She had lost the deep awareness of her Indigenous authenticity that had come to her in the pounding of the big drums and the chanting at the powwow in the SkyDome, and she wanted it back. Marrying the right First Nation, Métis, or Inuit man and raising Indigenous children in their Native culture, she decided, would do exactly that.

One day, reading the offerings on a dating site, she saw a posting from someone matching that profile:

> Métis man, early twenties, in master's program at
> Carleton University, seeks long-term relationship,
> perhaps matrimony, with Indigenous female soul-
> mate to discuss good books, to take long walks
> together, to watch NHL hockey games on TV, to
> drink good wine, and to listen to classical music.
> Particularly interested in exchanging views on his-
> tory and culture of our people in Canada. Depth
> of soul is more important than good looks.

Brenda called Greg, and they agreed to meet. When he walked into the coffee shop, she was immediately attracted by his rugged good looks and his buckskin jacket and braid. They sat and chatted for a while to become more at ease with each other. Then Brenda blurted out, "I'm a baby scooper survivor." She could see from his face that he didn't know what she was talking about.

Smiling with what he hoped Brenda would interpret as sympathy, Greg said, "Tell me about it."

Brenda assumed she was talking to a Métis who wasn't up-to-date on the issues roiling the Native community, so she decided to brief him. She told him about the collision between First Nations and Europeans beginning with the seventeenth-century arrival of Samuel de Champlain from France in what would become Canada and ending with the arrival of the baby scoopers in the 1960s. She spoke for over an hour, encouraged every so often by Greg, who sipped his coffee, fixed his gaze on her nose, and said, "Tell me about it."

By then Brenda was delighted, because she thought she had found the perfect Indigenous man who could help her discover her Indigenous female soul. Greg asked her why her birth mother had given her up, and she replied as if by rote, "My adoptive mother told me she didn't have enough money to provide for all her children, so she gave me up just after my birth so someone else could have the joy of welcoming me into their family."

"I don't believe that," Greg said.

"Neither do I," Brenda agreed, already under Greg's spell and playing the role of "yes" woman. But she didn't stop, and went on to tell him she had applied to the government to locate her birth mother and had found out that her adoption files were sealed, but a helpful official had looked into her case. After years of waiting, she had received a call from someone at the Yellow Dog First Nation who had identified herself as Raven Makwa, her younger sister. Raven had invited her to come and meet Maria, her mother, her father, Isaac, and her twin brother, Josh.

"Do you love your adoptive parents?" Greg asked.

"Of course, I do. They love me to this day, and we stay in touch with long letters and Christmas cards. I was lucky to be raised by people like them. They'd be there for me if I needed help, but we've moved on with our lives. Most of the kids taken into care spent their childhoods being shuffled from foster home to foster home, suffering from loneliness and abuse. Many of us come with deep-seated learning issues and end up as gang members on the streets. Not too many ended up in places like mine. I was lucky."

"Well, that's a mouthful," Greg said, interrupting her before she began talking about the plans for her visit to Yellow Dog.

"I'm sorry," Brenda said. "I always run on like that. I can't help myself. I get started and can't stop."

"Not to worry. I like it when people feel passionately about important matters."

After a pause, they turned to their university studies and how they had financed them. Greg let slip the fact that he had spent a summer working at a mine in northern Manitoba.

"Oh, please tell me about that job," Brenda said, anxious to keep the conversation going. "Tell me about your family and everything."

"No problem … if you have the time."

"I have the time," Brenda assured him. "My roommates know better than to wait up."

Greg hadn't been impressed when he first saw Brenda standing at the back of the café, smiling shyly like a wallflower at a singles' party waiting anxiously for someone, anyone, to end her misery and ask her to dance. He wouldn't have looked at her twice had he passed her on the street. He preferred tall, willowy, elegant women, and Brenda was somewhat on the short side with a round, comfortable body and a maternal face. Still, Greg was pleased to have stumbled across a walking encyclopedia on Indigenous issues who could lend credibility to his claim to be Métis.

Greg paused to consider what he needed from a wife. He wanted affection and trust — good looks and romantic Hollywood-style love weren't prerequisites. He wanted a woman like his mother who rarely questioned the judgment of his father, and who wouldn't complain if he occasionally slapped her around. He wanted someone to love him and wouldn't mind if he didn't love her back. He wanted a companion who would keep him from feeling lonely and believe him, or pretend to believe him, no matter how outrageous his lies were. But most of all, he wanted someone he could look at every day and be reminded of the Indian girl he had helped murder — sort of like a hair shirt on a medieval monk doing penance for past sins.

He decided to give a quick summary of his life and work at the Calvin mine. But he would use alternate facts so farfetched only someone who had met his list of requirements would believe or pretend to believe him. "My parents were good to me and wanted me to grow up with the Métis values of self-sufficiency, industriousness, and honesty. Though they lived in the modern world, they cherished the old ways," he continued, doing his best to suppress a smile. "Our ancestors hunted buffalo in the Red River Valley in Manitoba. They carried the trade goods of the Northwest and Hudson's Bay Companies in freighter canoes from Montreal to the head of the lakes and from there in smaller canoes all the way to trading posts in the Rocky Mountains. They then loaded their canoes and made their way back all the way to Montreal. They ate pounded buffalo meat mixed with berries, and the fish they caught and the ducks they shot. They were the masters of the wilds and they were my people."

"You're so lucky to know so much about your ancestors," Brenda said.

"That's not the half of it. In addition to passing on the history of my people, my parents used to take me up to Algonquin Park in the middle of the summer when I was barely ten. They'd paddle me up to some remote lake and leave me there for weeks at a time with no provisions and only a fishing line, a knife, and some matches. I actually loved those moments alone in the bush under the stars, except when black bears came calling."

"I've read that Indian boys and girls in the old days did things like that," Brenda said. "They'd build shelters in the bush and remain there fasting all by themselves until Gitche Manitou came to them in a dream to tell their futures. "By being adopted out, I missed that sort of thing. But what about your summers working in the mine? It must have been fascinating."

"I was coming to that. My parents had the money to cover my bills at university but wanted me to get a job and pay my own costs. That way I'd deepen my self-sufficiency. So, just after I graduated from high school, I got a job working at a rock face a thousand metres deep in a gold mine called the Calvin way up in northern Manitoba. The work was hard and dirty, but the pay was excellent and I made a lot of friends, especially a Métis brother by the name of Hubert. He used to take me to a fascinating tavern called the Zoo. It was called that because it had a real zoo with lions and tigers and peacocks and parrots and other things in cages near the entrance. The kids from the nearby First Nation used to spend their Sundays there because the management installed some pretty good playground equipment."

"Lucky kids," Brenda said. "Some people are so generous."

"That's right. Fortunately, the good people in this world out-number the bad ones."

"Keep on with your story. I find it so inspiring."

"The tavern itself was a meeting place where whites and Indians got together to share drinks, listen to live country-and-western music, and joke and laugh together. Occasionally, someone would have too much to drink and be asked to leave, but there was never any violence or drunkenness. The miners and the local Indians got along really well, but it was a shame that the mine owners never hired Indians, even if they had no problem taking on Métis like me."

"I'm going to do something about that if ever get a chance," Brenda vowed.

"Me, too," Greg said. "The Métis and Indians need to stand together. To fight injustice whenever and wherever it concerns them. I'm going to do my part someday."

In the months to come, Greg and Brenda spent their weekends together, taking long walks in the Gatineau Hills, drinking good wines, listening to classical music, and discussing the history and culture of Canada's First Peoples. After a decent interval, Greg asked Brenda to marry him. She accepted because she refused to see his shortcomings. They set the wedding month for May in Barrie after Greg graduated with his master's degree from Carleton and before he reported for work in September as a trade officer in the foreign service.

All went well at the wedding ceremony held at the church Greg had attended when he lived at home. Marg, but not Larry, would have preferred he was marrying Crystal but were enchanted with Brenda when they met her. They thought her white buckskin outfit and Greg's fawn-coloured buckskin jacket were most appropriate for a wedding in which the bride-to-be was Indian. The reception and dinner held at a nice hotel specializing in such things on nearby Lake Simcoe was a great success. Large numbers of friends and family members, teammates from Greg's old hockey team, several of Larry's OPP and service club buddies, and a selection of Marg's teacher colleagues attended. Jean and Nelson McGregor were invited, but with the start of tourist season their motel was full and they couldn't get away. Larry gave an emotional speech that had the guests alternatively laughing and crying. Greg kissed the bride and had the first dance. There were tears of joy in Marg's eyes as she contemplated the loss of her baby boy to another woman.

Everyone thought Brenda looked ever so lovely in her buckskin wedding dress, as did Greg in his matching buckskin jacket. Many guests commented on how Greg had grown up to be ever so handsome, a credit to his parents, a self-starter who had paid for his own university costs by hard work in summer jobs and student loans, when his parents, truth be known, could have footed the bill had they wanted to. Greg, they thought, was so liberal-minded in choosing to marry an Indian despite all the prejudice there was. By that time, Marg had told everyone Greg had chosen to dress up in an Indian costume to make the nice Indian girl feel at home, and so no one commented on his strange attire. There was also, as was normal at such affairs, an awkward moment.

Brenda, who was meeting Greg's parents for the first time, made the mistake of believing that both or one of them had to be Métis since their son was Métis. "Where does your family come from?" she asked Marg during a free moment at the reception.

"Oh, from all around here," Marg replied. "Mainly in Simcoe County. My ancestors came from County Armagh in Northern Ireland — strong Orangemen, never missed the annual parade on July 12. That's when the representatives of Good King Billy routed the Papists at the Battle of the Boyne. But we don't hold with all that anti-Catholic prejudice today."

"No, I meant where are you really from?" Brenda asked.

"What do you mean? I just told you."

"Don't you know? Whenever two Aboriginal people meet for the first time, they always ask where the other person is from. We're always interested in knowing what community claims you. And your family must be Métis, since Greg is Métis."

"But our family isn't Métis. And it stands to reason Greg isn't either. Wherever did you get that idea?"

"He told me."

"Then he's out of his mind."

"He's really proud of his Native heritage," Brenda said. "And so am I. I was adopted out right after I was born and had trouble connecting with Chippewa kids. I felt something was missing and searched for my birth mother. She's from the Yellow Dog Reserve."

"Please stop and listen to me," Marg said, holding up her hand. "You're not making any sense. How did you two lovebirds get together, anyway?"

"We fell in love mainly because we share an Indigenous identity. I'm Indian and he's Métis."

Marg snorted. "Is that so? Didn't you hear me say there's no Métis blood in this family?" Turning to Greg, who had been listening to the exchange, she said, "Please tell this poor girl you were only joking when you told her that story. You're no more Métis than I am."

"No, I wasn't joking. I feel Métis and that's good enough for me."

"But I have copies of my family tree and your father's family tree, and there's no sign of any Indian or Métis blood in either of them."

"A hundred years ago white people deliberately suppressed information on Native ancestors from census forms. You're too ashamed to admit it, but I'm not."

"You can't tell people truths they don't want to hear," Marg said, walking away.

8

HOMECOMING

B renda sat in the Thunder Bay airport departure lounge with
Greg, waiting for the connecting flight to Yellow Dog and
thinking about the forthcoming meeting with her birth family. In
her imagination, Maria, her birth mom, threw open the door of
the family house and broke into tears of happiness, hugging her
and showering her with kisses, saying, "I missed you so. I thought
of you every day. I've dreamed of this moment for decades!"

Brenda then saw herself hug Maria back, sobbing uncontrol-
lably, too overcome with emotion to utter a word. A distinguished
older gentleman suddenly appeared with tears in his eyes to say he
was her father. Maria stepped aside, and Isaac, for it was indeed
her dad, Isaac, who was welcoming her, hugged her tenderly, saying he had thought of her every minute of every day of separ-
ation. He was saying that when the baby scoopers had arrived
he and Maria had fought them like wildcats and thrown them

out of their cabin, but the Children's Aid Society representatives had returned with reinforcements, overpowered them, and taken away his beloved babies.

Then Raven, whom she would have already met at the airport on arrival at Yellow Dog, stepped into the scene, for this particular fantasy had a happy ending. Raven was accompanied by a man in his mid-twenties who looked like a younger Graham Greene, star of *Dances with Wolves*, and without being told, she instinctively knew the handsome man was her twin brother, Josh. Because twins could communicate with each other telegraphically, couldn't they? Josh said that he had been raised in a caring white family who had sent him to university to become a teacher. He had returned home to Yellow Dog to reconnect with his Native heritage and to teach in the local school.

The airport public-address system interrupted this imaginary scenario by announcing that Wolfskin Airlines, flying to Yellow Dog First Nation with a stop at South Caribou First Nation, was ready for boarding. Brenda's attention shifted from the welcome she imagined awaited her at her birth parents' home at Yellow Dog to the adventure of travelling in a single-engine eight-passenger plane into the heart of her ancestral homeland. But she was disappointed when she glanced out the window after the plane left the built-up area around Thunder Bay and flew northward over the bush.

For years she had seen the usual television scenes of northern Ontario — the lakes, rivers, black spruce bush, big blue skies, smiling Native guides and happy fishermen holding aloft trophy pike and walleye — and thought it would be wonderful to live in such a paradise. But she found the black spruce bush, muskeg, hills, lakes, and rivers cold, foreign, and forbidding compared to the landscape around Orillia and Ottawa. There wasn't a house or even a cottage in sight, and she felt no connection to the land of her family and ancestors.

Ploughing relentlessly through the cloudless sky, the plane began to pitch and buck, jerking the passengers up and down and side to side, before making a sudden plunge for hundreds of metres until levelling off and shooting upward, then straightening again, only to begin the cycle of agony again and again. Brenda turned green and reached for an air-sickness bag. And just as she thought the plane was about to crash, the pilot spoke calmly on the intercom, telling the passengers to keep their seat belts fastened. They had encountered hot-air currents rising at different rates as the June sun heated land and lakes. Not to worry.

The plane approached the airport at South Caribou and landed on the gravel runway. Brenda, Greg, and the other passengers disembarked, some to join relatives and friends waiting to take them home, the rest to kill time until new passengers arrived for the last leg to Yellow Dog. But after they stood around outside for a few minutes swatting mosquitoes and blackflies, the pilot came over to say there would be a longer delay. A family of four going to Yellow Dog had been out fishing when their outboard motor broke down. The motor had been fixed and they were on their way but wouldn't be at the airport for at least two hours.

The other passengers pulled out cigarettes, lit up, and gossiped to pass the time. Brenda, urged on by Greg who was becoming bored, went to see the Wolfskin representative to ask for help to arrange a trip into the community to see the sights.

"I'm sure one of the local people would be happy to give you a free tour," the woman said.

"We're not asking for charity," Brenda said. "We'll pay the going rate."

"You must be from Indian Affairs to offer to pay like that."

"I work there, but we're travelling on personal business."

"Are you sure you're not from the Indian Affairs audit branch? Pretending to be on private business but really here to check the books at the band office?"

"What's it to you if I was?" Brenda asked. "Can you or can you not get us a taxi?"

"Don't get mad. You Indian Affairs people can't take a joke."

"But I already told you I'm not here on official Indian Affairs business."

"And it's obvious you're not from around here."

Ten minutes later the chief introduced himself to Brenda, demanding to know why Indian Affairs hadn't warned him of her impending arrival.

"Why won't anyone believe me?" Brenda asked. "I work at Indian Affairs, but my husband and I are just passing through on our way to Yellow Dog. We just want to see the local sights, since we have time to kill."

"What's your business in Yellow Dog?" the chief asked.

Brenda was uncertain whether the chief was being nosy or politely making small talk but gave him the benefit of the doubt. "I was born there, but Children's Aid took me from my family in 1972 during the Sixties Scoop. I'm on my way back to meet my birth parents.

"What's your family name?"

"Makwa. Maria and Isaac Makwa are my birth parents. And if you really want to know, I have a brother called Josh and a sister named Raven."

"I know your dad real good. He's been one of the biggest bootleggers up here for years. The chief up there has been trying to close him down, but Isaac outsmarts him every time."

If Brenda was surprised at this revelation, she didn't let on, and asked if someone could show them around. The chief offered to be their guide and couldn't have been nicer — Brenda thought he was making up for badmouthing her father. She and Greg squeezed into the seat beside him in his pickup truck, and he drove down a dusty road past a Catholic church with its steeple intact but with its windows broken and with gaping holes in the gables.

"Most people go to the Pentecostal church these days," the chief said by way of explanation.

Brenda paid close attention to life on the South Caribou First Nation, since this visit constituted her first encounter with the northern Ontario Indigenous life she would have shared with her people had she not been taken away. Cannibalized cars and trucks coated in dust from the unpaved streets stood on blocks in front of houses, and the houses themselves were a mix of new construction, older homes in need of repair, and windowless packing cases with stovepipes protruding from their roofs. Dogs ran through the community in packs, children rode bicycles and laughed and shouted at one another like kids having fun everywhere in the world. Pickup trucks were on the move between the band office, the nursing station, and the co-op store. Teenagers played softball on a diamond behind the school. Men were at working building an addition to the school, and a crowd of kids were gathered behind the arena smoking cigarettes. When asked, the chief told her the small teepees behind the houses were smokehouses to preserve fish, moose meat, and geese. The people still relied on game for much of their food.

The chief was proud of his community despite its shortcomings and took them to visit the newly built pumping station that was providing clean water to the people for the first time in decades. He showed them the jail where three young people arrested and incarcerated for drunkenness had burned to death the previous winter when the building caught fire and police couldn't find the keys to the cells. The chief took them to the school and told them it lacked a library and gym and was built on land contaminated by an oil spill.

After that he took them to the co-op grocery store, and they walked the aisles and saw bacon at twelve dollars a pound, milk at fifteen dollars a jug, and bottled water at one hundred dollars a flat.

Brenda told him she would prepare a report and send it to senior management for follow-up when she returned to Ottawa. She didn't say that it was unlikely anything would be done, but the chief knew that already.

The last stop was the nursing station where the overworked nurse practitioner on duty laughed when Brenda asked her to describe the quality of health services.

"What's so funny?" Brenda asked.

"I'd rather laugh than cry," the nurse said. "For starters, the system is rigged against the Indians, and it's been that way from the beginning.

Brenda interrupted her to say she worked for Indian Affairs and everyone there was under the impression things were getting better.

"That's a lie, and I know what I'm talking about," the nurse said. "In South Caribou alone, three children under the age of fourteen killed themselves over the winter, despite telling everyone what they were planning to do. After the fact, the chief pleaded with Ottawa to send in mental health workers to provide counselling, but he didn't receive an answer, and more kids died. And that's not all. A senior citizen came in for help because of an asthma attack and died because the supplies of oxygen ran out. Children died from strep throat infections because Ottawa wouldn't provide funding for medications. Others died from rheumatic fever, diabetes, and hepatitis C because there isn't a resident doctor in the community. These things don't happen in white towns."

Brenda thanked the nurse and left with the chief and Greg for the airport. There was nothing she could say.

* * *

Greg and Brenda left South Caribou around three o'clock and arrived at Yellow Dog an hour later. Raven was there in a pickup truck to meet them. The sisters were wary of each other, even though they went through the expected motions of long-lost siblings — hugs and kisses and compliments. They were feeling their way, neither of them knowing quite what to expect from the other.

Brenda could tell that Raven didn't like Greg from the start. She laughed at his buckskin jacket and asked him if he was planning to attend a powwow. Brenda knew Greg didn't appreciate Raven's humour, but he didn't say anything, so Raven upped the stakes, telling Brenda to sit beside her in the cab and ordering Greg to sit on the spare tire in the box. "I need some private time with my sister." Greg ignored her, though, and pushed his way into the cab with them.

"There's a few things you need to know before you meet the parents," Raven said before putting the pickup in gear. Then she drove to a nearby hill and led them to a lookout where they could talk. The view was splendid. In one direction, Brenda saw the airport they had just left, with its tiny two-room terminal building, a plane landing, and a cluster of pickup trucks and people waiting to meet the new passengers who would soon be disembarking and heading to their homes. From off in the distance in another direction, she heard children playing and laughing, just as they had at South Caribou.

Raven poked Brenda to get her attention and pointed across the river to an expanse of land filled with the blackened skeletons of trees and new growth. "Years ago, a forest fire raced down the slope toward the community. But at the last minute it stopped at the river's edge and burned itself out. There was a bright side, though. The people now get their firewood from the dead trees and haul it home in the winter on sleds attached to their snowmobiles."

"Is there anything left of the old Yellow Dog?" Brenda asked.

Raven pointed to the cluster of buildings that made up the modern reserve. "The one that was here when you and Josh were born is long gone. Even the elders of that period who tried to keep the old ways alive are dead. The Indian agent left to be replaced by elected chiefs and councils responsible for the day-to-day management of the community. The population exploded from three hundred to twelve hundred, and an all-weather road now leads from the south past Yellow Dog to the site of a future chromite mine in Ontario's Ring of Fire mineral development."

"What else has changed?"

"Lots of things. The people now travel out by car or truck to Pickle Lake, Thunder Bay, or Sioux Lookout to spend their child allowances, pensions, paycheques, and welfare payments at the shopping centres. Wives stock up on detergent, toilet paper, Pampers, and pasta that cost a fraction of what's charged at the local co-op. Husbands buy used pickups and drive them home. The young guys spend their time drinking in the bars until they run out of money and are tossed out."

"Are the houses in Yellow Dog in as bad shape as the ones at South Caribou?"

"They're about the same," Raven said. "They're pretty much the same on First Nations up here in the North. Decaying homes, band offices, and the like in all our communities up here have become the new normal. We complain but know they won't be fixed up or replaced in our lifetimes."

"The nurse practitioner at South Caribou told us three children killed themselves over there during the winter. Is it the same here?"

"It's the same here and everywhere in the North. It's heartbreaking, especially for the parents among the residential school survivors. They're now in their fifties, sixties, and seventies and have to live with the knowledge that they bear part of the blame for being such bad parents."

Before Brenda could ask any more questions, Raven said, "I sometimes get so mad at them. Most are doing the best they can for their kids. But getting drunk and doing drugs, no matter how much you suffered at residential school or being a victim of the Sixties Scoop, is no excuse for poor parenting. A few trips with their kids out to the delights of Pickle Lake, Thunder Bay, or Sioux Lookout doesn't compensate for poor parenting. Healing circles in which the grown-ups confess their mistakes raising their kids and promise to do better don't make up for poor parenting. Weeping and crying at funeral services for their children doesn't make up for poor parenting. We've got to take responsibility for our actions."

Raven told Brenda that she was still a kid when she first saw through the hypocrisy of the older generation, who avoided responsibility by blaming everyone else for their poor parenting. "Our own mother was one of the worst. I spent my childhood listening to her moaning about her loneliness at residential school, and all the while she didn't have time for me."

Brenda took Raven in her arms. "I had no idea. I don't know what to say."

Raven hugged her back. "There's more. I spent those early years acting out, raising hell with the other kids, painting graffiti on walls, smashing the windows of the school and band office, trashing empty houses, cutting myself with razors, sniffing gasoline, and drinking booze bought from our own father, the community bootlegger. And when I just couldn't take it anymore, I joined a suicide pact, tied one end of a rope high on the branch of a tree and the other around my neck, and jumped. That's one of the favourite ways kids use to kill themselves."

Waiting for a moment to give Brenda time to absorb everything she had said, Raven continued. "But the rope broke, and as I was lying half-dead on the ground waiting for someone to help me to the nursing station, I decided I no longer wanted to die just because

Maria and Isaac were such rotten parents. I know it sounds melo-dramatic, but it's the truth. They wouldn't have missed me, anyway.

"So I got together with a few other kids who thought like me and we decided to take matters into our own hands, agreed not to take crap from anyone who stood in our way, became activists, campaigned for a new school, for more and better suicide pre-vention counselling, breakfasts for hungry schoolchildren, a drug rehabilitation study, and a program to take troubled youth out on the land to find themselves with elders. We managed to shame Indian Affairs into providing a new school but not the other pro-grams. And when the time came, some of us left home to see if we could bring about change from the outside. I'm now enrolled in a general arts program at Lakehead University, scheduled to begin in the fall. Not bad coming from a messed-up family!"

Maria was drunk and crying when she met them at the door and fled to her room when Brenda tried to embrace her. Raven squeezed Brenda's hand and said, "Don't mind Maria. She has her good and bad days, and this is one of the bad ones. She's probably forgotten she invited you here and didn't know who you are."

Brenda's meeting with Isaac didn't go any better. He was in the living room sitting in an armchair with a baseball cap stuck on his head at an angle and wearing a dirty undershirt. He had a beer in one hand, a TV remote in the other, and was studiously watching the Toronto Blue Jays play the Baltimore Orioles on satellite tele-vision. He said nothing when Raven tried to tell him his first-born daughter was home at last, and when she bent over to kiss him, he pushed her away without taking his eyes off the screen. The reunion couldn't have been worse. Brenda was shattered.

Fortunately, Brenda clicked with Josh, her twin brother. Heavily tattooed and muscular with dark brown scarred skin, black

eyes, and braided hair, he came out of a back room, took her in
his arms, and said, "Welcome home, sis. I hope you won't be too
disappointed with the way you were received. And welcome to you,
as well, whoever you are." He shook hands with Greg, who had
come in carrying their pack.

Raven stepped forward with a suggestion to organize the
homecoming. "Let's leave our overjoyed parents to do their thing
and get to know each other over mugs of tea."

Josh helped Raven lead the way outside, carrying a tray with
mugs and a pot of tea to a picnic table in a gazebo overlooking
the river. Brenda stumbled along, not paying attention to where
she was going, more shocked than disappointed at the indifferent
verging on hostile reception accorded to her by Maria and Isaac.

*How could I have been so stupid to have assumed my birth parents
would have welcomed me back into their family, that they would have
wanted to meet me as much as I wanted to meet them?* she thought.
When, in fact, they couldn't have cared less!

Raven set down the tray on the table in the gazebo and went
back to get Brenda, who was looking around outside but seemed
to have forgotten what she was doing and why she was even there.

"Come sit with me," Raven said, taking Brenda by the arm, leading her to a seat, and installing her beside her. "I can only imagine
how upset you must be to learn the truth about our parents."

"There's lots of things I'm going to have to rethink," Brenda said
as Raven served her a mug of tea. "For instance, I always thought
they didn't want to give me up when the Children's Aid came for
me when I was a baby. Maybe they were happy to get rid of me."

"Me, too," Josh said. "Don't forget we were taken away
together."

"Maybe I should be glad a white couple adopted me and raised
me as a daughter!" Brenda said.

Raven said nothing, letting the others do the talking.

"What sort of person would I have turned out to be if I hadn't been taken away?" Brenda asked, speaking to Raven. "I probably would have killed myself if I had suffered like you through a life with parents like Maria and Isaac. I know myself. I'm weak. I wouldn't have bounced back from a failed suicide attempt and contributed to society like you did. I'm just sorry it's taken so long to learn the truth — so many years wasted worrying about nothing!"

"Don't be so hard on yourself, sis," Josh said. "By the sound of it, you had a lot going for you with decent adoptive parents, an education, a good job, and a purpose in life."

"How about you, Josh? What sort of adoptive family did you end up with?" Brenda asked.

"My adoptive family was a Native gang."

Thinking he was joking, Brenda started to laugh but stopped when she saw he was serious.

"I grew up in Winnipeg's Native ghetto and was shuffled from one abusive home to another by foster parents who took in kids for the payments they received from the child welfare people. Then I almost killed a guy in a street fight and ended up in the Rocky Mountain Pen. That's where I met members of a Native gang and we all looked out for each other. We came from similar backgrounds. They were the only family I ever knew up to then."

"Tell Brenda how you managed to give up that way of life," Raven said to Josh.

"I became an enforcer for my gang in fights against other Native gangs in prison until some older Native inmates pulled me aside and told me I'd spend the rest of my life on the inside unless I got my act together." Speaking directly to Brenda, who gave him her full attention, Josh continued. "I began to hang out with my new friends who taught me the importance of Native pride and convinced me to take part in healing circles and sweat lodge ceremonies. That turned my life around. The parole board located our birth parents and tried to release me early into their care, but Maria and Isaac wanted nothing to do with me. I eventually served my time and went to Yellow Dog to live with them, anyway, whether they liked it or not. It was a good decision. I've now met both of my sisters, and one is an outsider like me."

9

RAVEN'S DIARY

JUNE 27, 1996
YELLOW DOG

Woke up this morning glad to be alive but wasn't happy when I pulled open the curtains to find Elijah Wawanosh once again leering at me from his window. He's the only guy around here who frightens me like that. Elijah and I go back a long, uneasy way. He used to live over on the other side of the community, but he took a fancy to me. When I was just a little girl of six, he got me alone and offered me a candy, and when I reached over to get it, he picked me up and touched my private parts. What a pig! Never mentioned it to my mother. She'd just cry some more and do nothing. Since that time, he's stalked me. Eventually, he threw up a shack only a couple of metres from our house. Too bad there isn't a building code on Yellow Dog to stop people from building wherever they want. He hasn't had the decency to put curtains and blinds on the windows.

Year after year he's been there, staring at my window, keeping me prisoner, smoking roll-your-own cigarettes, and waiting for me to open my curtains. Even at night I can feel his presence in the dark. Maybe he's hoping I'll give him a sign of some sort, maybe some indication I love him or at least accept him. Who knows? I once tried to be nice to him, thinking he would stop it if I said something agreeable. I was about thirteen and ran into him on the road in front of our house. I only said hello, but he looked away as if he'd been caught in a lie.

When a couple of women from around here went missing, he disappeared, as well, and didn't come back for months. I thought there was some connection but kept my thoughts to myself. Wouldn't do to go around accusing people of big crimes when you have no proof and everybody's related to everyone else. Would just set family on family and there'd be bloodshed. I still don't like it when he calls out to me when there's no one around and asks, "Want another candy?" followed by that sick laugh of his. He's a strange one, for sure. I've thought about telling Josh but never have because he'd beat Elijah to death, for sure. I wouldn't want that on my conscience. The guy's obviously not all there.

JUNE 28, 5:00 A.M.

Sun's shining and today's the day Brenda and her creep of a husband will be leaving. Hurrah! It's not Brenda who's the problem, though she's too nice for her own good. Always agreeing with him no matter what idiocy he comes up with. For instance, when I gave him the numbers for the suicides and murders up north that resulted from herding kids into residential schools and from the 1960s Scoop, he said those things happened in the past and the Canadians of today shouldn't be blamed for what had taken place years ago.

He didn't like it when I told him he didn't know his history. Baby scooping dragged on until the 1980s, and the last residential school in Canada closed its doors in the early 1990s. Even today tens of thousands of Indian kids in care are being treated as second-class citizens. I said many of the politicians in office in Ottawa and the provinces approved these policies and needed to be held accountable, as should every Canadian voter who had supported these measures, which could only be called racist.

Brenda tried to change the subject because she knew I was winning the argument, but Greg got red in the face and dug himself in deeper, saying the white people of today shouldn't be blamed for the terrible things done to Indians in the nineteenth century, like taking their lands, starving them, and treating them like subhumans under the *Indian Act*. The people responsible for those things have been dead for years. Besides, that was the way everyone treated Indians in those days.

"Maybe you can blame history," he'd said, "but it wasn't the fault of the white people then or now."

I asked him whose side he was on, anyway. "Aren't you Metis? Don't you defend your people?"

"I'm proud of my white and Indian ancestors," he said. "And I do my best to be intellectually honest."

I got mad and said I thought anyone Métis or not who defended the behaviour of white colonialism whenever or wherever it takes place should also be held accountable. Brenda stepped in on Greg's side to tell me she supported her husband and couldn't we talk about something else.

I told Brenda to butt out, that we were discussing important matters. "You're the one with the fancy university degrees," I said to Greg. "You must have heard of William Faulkner, the American author, talking about the American South after the Civil War. He said, 'The past is never dead. It's not even past.' That means you can't separate the past from the present no matter how much people like you try."

Greg shook his head and said I was relying on an obscure quotation from an author from another time to support an untenable argument. I told him that if he wanted examples I could give them and said, "When Canada's chief of diplomacy, Lester Pearson, won the Nobel Peace Prize in the 1950s, the police were still hauling Indian kids off to residential schools. When Pierre Trudeau was prime minister in the 1970s, the child welfare agencies were taking Indian babies, like Brenda and Josh, from their mothers. You can't tell me these distinguished Canadian politicians hadn't inherited at least some of the racist attitudes of their ancestors."

Our little dust-up ended at that point, and we moved on to other things. But it was strange for Brenda to take his side. Maybe she was afraid of him. He doesn't scare me, though, even if his eyes are like those of a wolf — sly and mean and insisting on getting his own way no matter what. His stare reminds me of Elijah's. Like a mad dog after a wounded deer, just wanting to kill and not to eat. Like a maniac after someone to hurt, maybe rape and maybe kill, always quiet but in a sullen way, making everybody nervous and making it clear he'd rather be somewhere else.

Then again it could have just been cultural shock, not just for Greg but for Brenda, too. They weren't used to using an outhouse, or the clouds of blackflies and deer flies that make life miserable. They didn't like it on the first night when the neighbours walked in without knocking and stared at them as if they were visitors from Mars. It must have been a shock to Brenda when she found out her dad was a bootlegger with a lot of appreciative customers.

I also think there's something more fundamental at play here. When we were alone, she asked me why I just didn't leave the North with its problems of suicide, terrible schools, open prejudice, police violence, family breakdown, and extreme poverty for southern Ontario. Native people would still run into problems of being accepted, but the schools were better, health care better, and there was lots of work for anyone who went on to college or university. People's lives would be so much easier.

I told her all those things could well be true, but I loved the North, including Yellow Dog with all its problems. I'd never feel at home anywhere else, like in Ottawa or Toronto. The farthest south I could live would be Thunder Bay despite its racism. She said she understood but probably didn't. She said I felt that way because I was raised here and couldn't live anywhere else. I told her it was more complicated than that. The North has been the homeland of our people for ten thousand years. For ten thousand years our ancestors prayed to the unseen power that runs through the land, lakes, rivers, sky, and all things, animals, stones, water, animate and inanimate. That power, the power of Manitou, binds everything together in a holy universe. Many of us still feel the power and believe we're part of the land and should never leave it. That's why I'll be buried up here beside our parents, even if they've been rotten parents. I think Brenda still didn't get it.

It's now six o'clock, and I can hear Greg yelling at Brenda and Brenda crying. I wish she'd never married him. Why does she take it? In another bedroom, I can hear my mother coughing. Soon she'll push herself out of bed and stagger to the kitchen to pour herself a drink — straight no mix. In a few minutes, Isaac will make his way out to join her, and they'll spend the rest of the day drinking. They've been alcoholics for as long as I can remember. They'll soon get down on their knees and pray to God for strength to face the day. They make me sick. They're terrible parents, but I don't blame them, even though they should take responsibility for their actions. Something happened at residential school that my mother never wants to talk about. Schools like that are now closed in Canada, thank God. They'll eventually get a big cheque and an apology from the government, but they're damaged for life. People like them who went to those schools shouldn't be allowed to have kids. I know that from personal experience.

It's now noon, and they've left with Isaac in his truck for the airport. Lots of drama before departure that won't soon be forgotten. First, Greg got mad at Brenda for taking too much time with the packing and slapped her. Then she apologized to him for being slow and said it would never happen again. Josh wasn't around, and I didn't want to butt in, in case it didn't help matters. Brenda saw me looking on and lowered her eyes. That's when I realized she was a battered woman.

Things went downhill when everyone except Maria went outside to say goodbye. By that time, Josh had come back, and feeling the tension in the air, asked what was going on. I couldn't keep my big mouth shut and said Greg had slapped our sister. Isaac thought it was funny and said maybe she deserved it. Brenda said it was nothing, but Josh gave Greg a thrashing and said if he ever harmed his sister again he'd cut off his balls. Maria then came out, handed Brenda a letter, and went back inside without saying a word. Brenda was already crying when she climbed into the truck. I wouldn't have wanted to be a passenger on that ride to the airport.

10

MARIA'S LETTER

To Brenda,

There's a few things I won't be able to tell you to your face when you come next week. That's the reason I've written this letter to give to you when you leave. You must wonder why I didn't stop the Children's Aid people from taking you away from me when you were a baby. But the fact of the matter is I was glad to get rid of you and your brother, too. Times were tough, and there weren't no money coming in and fishing and hunting and trapping was bad. My folks helped us out and shared their catches with us as well as a little flour, lard, and tea to keep us going. But we were always short of food, and it was hard to nurse you and your brother. It was either give you to the white people or watch you get sick.

But there's something else, a secret so awful I won't never be able to tell you about it to your face. You probably heard about those residential schools and how cruel and bad the teachers were. The beatings, the rapes, and all those awful things. Well, I had to put up with ten years of pure hell in one of them. Screwed me up for good. Could hardly read and write and cook when they let me out, despite all those years of schooling. Didn't know how to talk to people and fit for nothing. Only thing I could do was drink. It's no secret those white teachers and staff abused us Indian kids, hitting and making us do things with them, sexual things I'm too ashamed to mention. It went on for years and years, and there weren't nothing nobody could do to stop it. I'll never forgive those bastards.

But you probably never knew the big Indian boys did the same thing to the Indian girls, and that was worse because the touching and raping came from our own people. They didn't care if you were a cousin or a friend. They did it just the same all the time week after week, month after month, year after year. We had nobody to turn to for help. I left the school for good at sixteen, pregnant with you and Josh by Isaac. He was a student at that school just like me and came from Yellow Dog just like me. I knew him all my life. Our folks knew each other and made us get married, but I hated him then and I hate him now. He has no respect for me and beats me all the time. But I wait till he's drunk and clobber him with a piece of firewood.

I hated you and Josh since you were born from rape. Maybe that's why I said nothing and didn't try to stop them when they came for you and your brother. Maybe that's why I didn't want Josh to live with us when he showed up here, begging for a place to stay after he got out of jail. That's why I didn't want you to come visit. Raven made me say yes. It's not your fault, but don't come back.

— Maria

PART 4

DISCREDITABLE CONDUCT
1996–2017

THE TRADE COMMISSIONER

Greg was in for a disagreeable surprise when Departmental Security Officer Mike McFadden asked him to drop every-thing and come to see him. "I know you've received a job offer and are supposed to report for work in a few weeks' time," he said, "but the Ottawa police sent me a report saying you've been seen hanging around the market late at night talking to hookers. It's common knowledge that that area is a hangout for low-lifes and that all those hookers are Indians. You better have a good excuse for consorting with people like that or you won't be working here."

"I haven't been 'hanging around' the market late at night. I've lived there for years. Lots of respectable middle-class people live there. I'm also an Indigenous person, and my wife is Indigenous, and so are many of our friends. Maybe they saw me talking to them. Are you really saying all Indigenous people are low-life sex workers? If so, can I quote you? That's a racist comment."

Mike shrugged, and Greg reported for work on schedule. His superiors were properly impressed with the depth of his knowledge on the big international issues of the day but grew tired of receiving unsolicited recommendations on how to change Canadian foreign policy for the better. And, as sometimes happened in these cases, to punish his excess of zeal, they didn't promote him when his probationary period ended two years later. However, they did grant his request to be sent as a junior trade commissioner to Havana when a position opened up in the summer of 1998. It didn't bother Greg that Cuba was going through hard economic times after the end of Russia's massive aid program following the collapse of the Soviet Union in 1991. He was still looking forward to meeting Fidel Castro, his hero.

In a sign of growing tensions in their marriage, Greg hadn't bothered to consult Brenda about the posting beforehand. He merely told her to quit her job, pack up their possessions, and be ready to move by the end of the summer. Brenda didn't object, even though moving from Canada meant leaving a job she liked, friends she had made in Ottawa, and her newly discovered brother and sister. Her trip to Yellow Dog had left her depressed, and she wanted to get away for a while, a long while, to come to terms with what she had seen and heard. She had known that living conditions in the North for Indigenous people were terrible, but that fact hadn't registered emotionally. She had encountered the Third World and didn't like it at all.

Even though he was happy enough to be going to Cuba, Greg derived no pleasure from the late-evening flight to Havana in early September. He was still bitterly disappointed at not being promoted when in his opinion he was smarter than any of the officers who had joined the department with him. To make matters worse, the toilets on the ancient Russian-built passenger turboprop were filled to the top with a stinking mix of chemicals and excrement that slopped over onto the floor and ran out under the door into the aisle whenever turbulence was encountered. The crew were surly and the seats were marked by coffee stains, spilt wine, and cigarette burns. Discipline was breaking down, and it was everyone for himself in post-Soviet Cuba.

The plane was filled with happy Canadians and their scream-ing, poorly disciplined kids on their way to holiday on Cuba's beaches. The crew had started handing out free rum as soon as the plane was airborne, and it hadn't taken long for the passengers to begin singing and quarrelling. When Greg and Brenda declined their invitation to join in the festivities, their fellow Canadians took it badly and made sarcastic comments about Greg's buckskin jacket and braid.

"Going to a Wild West show?" one of them asked.

"As Wild Bill Hickok?" another added, and everyone thought that witticism was hysterically funny.

"And you," someone else asked Brenda, who was recognizably First Nation despite being dressed in a conservative business outfit, "you going as Pocahontas?"

Everyone laughed again.

Greg was offended and made the mistake of trying to pull rank, telling them with an air of self-importance that he was a member of Canada's foreign service on his way to take up a diplomatic appointment at Canada's Havana embassy. "Show a little respect," he said, but that just touched off another wave of laughter.

Brenda whispered to him, "Let it go. They'll soon get tired of us and find something else to keep themselves amused."

Greg turned on her, slapping and punching her the way he did back in Ottawa, ignoring the outraged calls to lay off from the people in the aisle, whose mood had changed from merriment to concern that they were dealing with a madman dressed up as an Indian. To be sure, Greg wasn't abusing Brenda because she was an Indian. He had long ago recognized that Indians, Métis, and Inuit were people like any other Canadian, white, black, brown, or yellow, and all the colours in between. They were human beings just as he was with their strengths and frailties, their streaks of good and bad. He was slapping her around for the same reasons his father beat up his mother on Saturday nights after the Toronto Maple Leafs lost a hockey game — because he was filled with rage and disappointment and because he was seeking an outlet for his frustrations.

Havana was in darkness as the plane circled prior to landing. The country was suffering through its seventh year of hard economic times since the collapse of the Soviet Union. The Canadian ambassador had reported that the government was still finding it challenging to keep the lights on. There were long line ups for scarce food at the ration shops, and fewer vintage 1940s and 1950s cars on the roads. The buses had been replaced by huge farm tractors hauling a half-dozen or more wagons crammed with passengers standing up and holding tightly to one another to keep from falling off.

No planes were waiting on the tarmac, and the pilot went directly to the gate. A flight attendant opened the door, and hot, heavy, humid air poured in, accompanied by the smell of melting tar, frangipani, and garbage. Sweat oozed from Greg's every pore, soaking his shirt and rendering him suddenly weary and longing for strong espresso. The cabin crew abandoned the passengers and rushed out the door and down the stairs, carrying Cuban rum and cigars purloined from the galley. Someone from the embassy showed up and drove them to their staff quarters past mansions falling into ruin and women in spandex pants and low-cut blouses selling their bodies under the faint light of the few street lights. It was a scene from a Gabriel García Márquez novel, and Greg took careful note of the women for future reference.

Ambassador Horace Quigley was a bachelor on his last posting who had served at small embassies and high commissions on all habitable continents. He lived in an opulent six-bedroom residence, tastefully decorated by experts from headquarters, with an Olympic-size swimming pool, a tennis court with night lighting, and six household staff. They did the laundering and cleaning, made the beds, cut the grass, tended the flower gardens, prepared sit-down dinners for up to two dozen guests, buffet lunches for up to two hundred, receptions for up to a thousand, and discreet dinners for four with President Castro himself. One of their responsibilities, which they didn't bother to conceal, was to provide regular reports on the ambassador and his Canada-based staff to MININT, the sinister Ministry of the Interior. And one of MININT's roles was to blackmail diplomats like Greg into handing over the secrets of their countries.

Canada's relations with Cuba were neither good nor bad. Canada maintained an embassy in Havana mainly because Washington had once ordered it to close down. At the top, Castro didn't like capitalists. Canada was a capitalist country, but the Cuban leader overlooked Canada's political orientation because his country needed goods and services available nowhere else. Since he was surrounded by "yes" men and was lonely in his palace, he often visited Ambassador Quigley to spend the night eating imported Canadian turkey dinners and reminiscing about the good old days before revolutionary Cuba went broke.

But a mini-crisis was developing that could put at risk this privileged if tenuous personal relationship: they were running out of topics to talk about. The ambassador had been in Cuba for five years, and Castro had visited him dozens of times, each stint lasting an average of between six to eight hours. They had discussed ad nauseam the failings of the United States; revolution in Central America; national liberation movements in Africa; the respective merits of Cuban langoustes and Prince Edward Island lobsters; the Cuban cigar and rum industries; the Cuban health and education system; the latest Cuban international triumphs in track and field, baseball, and basketball; the sugar harvest; North Korea's nuclear armaments program; Haitian and Cuban voodoo practices; and globalization. Castro had let his boredom show, and there was a risk he would stop coming to the Canadian residence and spend his evenings with the Swedes. Canada would lose face. What was the ambassador to do?

The arrival of Greg wearing his buckskin jacket provided a solution. Castro was interested in the plight of marginalized people wherever they could be found, wasn't he? Canada's Indigenous people were marginalized people, weren't they? The junior Canadian trade commissioner was an Indigenous person, wasn't he? Ambassador Quigley invited his new trade commissioner to join him the next time the president came for dinner. His task was to provide the views of a marginalized Canadian diplomat on the situation of the marginalized Indigenous people in Canada to Fidel Castro. Castro wouldn't be bored and would continue to attend Ambassador Quigley's dinners, and everyone would be happy.

But when the evening arrived and it was Greg's turn to speak, he was so awestruck at being in the presence of the great man himself he couldn't say a word. Castro ended his dinner dates with Canada's ambassador and started spending time with the Swedes. Fortunately, for Greg, it turned out that Quigley didn't really mind. As an older gentleman, he much preferred drinking a hot rum toddy and going to bed early to staying up until four in the morning listening to Castro rant and rave and repeat himself about the nasty United States.

As time passed, Greg was promoted from third to second secretary, but his pay went up by only five hundred dollars a year before tax. But one evening the telephone rang at his staff quarters. Brenda answered. A woman, who wouldn't give her name, was on the line wanting to speak to Greg. Brenda passed the telephone to her husband, who was greeted by a sexy voice saying she was one of his many admirers and wanted to meet him. The departmental security officer had warned Greg about such calls, saying they were always from MININT agents seeking to entrap foreign diplomats. But Greg was disgruntled and prepared to take risks. Perhaps a beautiful woman offering sex and money in exchange for information? He had a score to settle with the department! He decided to see what was on offer.

A tall, slim, olive-skinned woman in her mid-twenties, who said her name was Neurka, met him on the beach. Although Greg should have known better, he accompanied her to a government bungalow and spent the night with her. His expectations hadn't been high, thinking she was just another prostitute from MININT's stable of women. However, she turned out to be an English-speaking Havana university graduate in history and art appreciation who was Brenda's opposite in every respect. Neurka smiled all the time and was ready to joke around; Brenda was always downcast. Neurka was proud to be Cuban; Brenda was proud to be Indigenous but not Canadian. Neurka could play the cello; Brenda knew only the fiddle. Neurka had visited the Hermitage Museum, Lenin's Tomb, and Yasnaya Polyana, the country home of Tolstoy, during a visit to Russia; Brenda hadn't. She had met Che Guevara; Brenda hadn't. Greg was smitten.

Then somebody named Raúl Cárdenas invited him to lunch, saying he worked for a state enterprise interested in doing business with Canada. Greg accepted, and after his host insisted he be called Raúl, they sat down to an excellent lunch and talked politely about nothing in particular. Getting down to business over coffee, Raúl said, "You've probably guessed by now that I'm really from MININT."

After Greg smiled and said nothing, Raúl smiled back and said, "One of our responsibilities is to cultivate visitors to our country who have shown great sensitivity to Cuba's national aspirations."

"Isn't this the moment when you're supposed to show me the pictures?" Greg asked, his smile gone. "Of Neurka and me in bed? Naked? To get me to work for you? Is that the way these things work?"

"We have such pictures," Raúl said, likewise becoming serious as the negotiations began. "I'll send you a set, but would never show them to anybody else."

"I assume Neurka works for you."

"In fact, she does. She's a loyal comrade."

"Then I suppose I have no choice."

"But, of course, you have a choice. We would never ask you to do anything that violated your principles."

"Would I be able to continue seeing her?"

"If that's your wish. She's fond of you."

"What am I supposed to do?"

"Nothing much. Just make copies of the classified documents that come over your desk and give them to Neurka, who will give them to me. So, what do you say? Are you going to work for us or not?"

"I'll do it only as long as I can see Neurka."

The two men shook hands, and Greg was entrapped.

The next time Greg saw Neurka she gave him a miniature camera and showed him how to use it. Throughout his posting, Greg photographed copies of Canadian diplomatic mail and other secret documents. With the information he provided, MININT rounded up and threw into jail local human-rights activists and penetrated Canada's embassy to place listening devices in its most sensitive areas. Before visits of Canadian ministers, MININT was reading their briefing books. Soon after Canada's prime minister met with the American president in the White House, Castro was reading a summary of their deliberations. After the heads of Canada's security services met with their American counterparts to discuss anti-terrorist operations, their conclusions were being studied by the Chinese.

Greg was unaware just how much harm he was causing, but even if he had known, he wouldn't have cared. He was so infatuated with Neurka that he would have done anything to please her. A year into their relationship he found the courage to tell her that he loved her and wanted to leave the foreign service, divorce his wife, marry her, and live in Cuba. She didn't laugh, but said they came from different worlds and he would never fit into hers. In the meantime, they should make the best of their time together. Greg didn't raise the matter with her again but was deeply hurt.

Just before the end of Greg's posting in July 2002, Raúl invited him to lunch and took a hard line, threatening to send the compromising photos with Neurka to his wife and to the department if he didn't work for MININT from Ottawa. Greg refused. Being an informant for MININT without Neurka held no appeal. He went home, and showed the photos to Brenda. She looked at Neurka's body and then at Greg but said nothing.

After his arrival in Ottawa, Greg showed the photos to Departmental Security Officer Mike McFadden and told the man he had met a woman who had enticed him to spend the night with him. MININT had secretly taken photos and tried to blackmail him. But being a loyal employee, he had, of course, refused.

"What's your wife say about this?" McFadden asked. "I assume you told her."

"I told her and she forgave me."

"Now what's the damage? How many times did you see her?"

"Just that once."

"What did you give them?"

"I handed over some press clippings and unclassified reports from our missions. But that was all."

"How much did they pay you?"

"Nothing, and I didn't ask for anything."

"Are you sure? That doesn't sound right."

"I would never hurt my country. In a moment of weakness, I betrayed my wife and country."

When McFadden met with representatives of the RCMP to review Greg's case, they assumed they were dealing with just another instance of an otherwise loyal departmental employee on a posting in a Communist country being enticed into a one-night stand. The RCMP went easy on employees who turned themselves in before they were caught, especially in a case like Greg's. Since they had no reason not to believe him, they told him he could keep his job but would never serve Canada abroad again.

Greg and Brenda started their new life in Ottawa by making a down payment on a three-bedroom bungalow in a middle-class neighbourhood. Brenda returned to her job at Indian Affairs to find out that the years had been good for the First Nations people of southern Ontario. In a process that had begun when she was still in high school in the 1980s and had accelerated throughout the 1990s, growing numbers of people were finding steady work in the booming local economy. New houses replaced the shacks of years gone by. Proper sewage and water infrastructure replaced outhouses. More and more people married out and brought their brides and husbands back to live on the First Nations where they were welcomed. Their children moved more easily between the white and Native worlds but almost always identified themselves as Indigenous in a display of Native pride. The gap between the quality of life on the First Nations in the North and those in the South that had existed for years was widening.

The department stuck Greg in a low-level, make-work job in Historical Division on some long-departed and marginal Canadian diplomat and forgot him when he reported for work after messing up in Havana. That was the institution's way of dealing with him for working for MININT. The punishment was harsher than he had expected and not just from departmental management. Word had gone around that he had betrayed the department, and for some people that was akin to letting down the nation itself. He was shunned. His old friends stopped speaking to him, and he had to eat by himself in the cafeteria, listening to his former colleagues at the surrounding tables tell tall delicious tales about the countries they had served in and all the great men and women they had met.

He used to enjoy attending the performances of the National Arts Centre Orchestra, but the first time he went back, strangers stared at him, so he never returned. A satirical magazine ran a story with a picture of Greg dressed in his Native garb entitled "Fake Métis a Traitor!" Greg tossed away the jacket, untied the braid, and resumed his white persona. By that time, Brenda knew he wasn't Native and made no comment. But Greg's parents cared, not about his flip-flop on identity but on his traitorous behaviour. After they got their hands on a copy of the magazine, he wasn't welcome back in Barrie.

Greg and Brenda grew closer for a while, but that didn't last. He began to have recurrent spells of depression accompanied by nightmares about killing the Indian girl mixed in with haunting dreams about the phoniness of the life he had been leading. By that time, Brenda had picked up her life where she had left it when she married Greg, but this time she made a point of making friends with people who had been adopted out during the Sixties Scoop and who had tried but failed to reconnect with their birth families and First Nations. Raven once came to visit, but she argued with Greg and didn't come back. Instead Brenda spent a week or two each year at her apartment in Thunder Bay where she worked at the university. Josh never came to visit in Ottawa, but she got together with him in Thunder Bay. Not wishing to be humiliated again, Brenda didn't try to see Maria and Isaac.

Brenda and Greg fell into a rut. She did the cooking and cleaning, cutting the grass in spring and summer and shovelling the snow in winter, while he read newspapers and thought about Neurka and her absence from his life … and about the bastards in the department who had denied him promotion before he'd left for Cuba. They could have afforded to have someone come in once a week to do the heavy lifting, but Greg said no. The place for women was in the house looking after their men. His mother did everything at home in Barrie, and Brenda would do the same. Brenda rarely smiled, unable to forget the photos of her husband and Neurka in bed in Cuba.

They woke up every morning in their separate beds to the sound of the seven o'clock CBC Radio news, rose, went to their separate bathrooms, did the necessary, returned and dressed, made and ate breakfast, and went to the bus stop without saying a word to each other. Brenda went to Indian Affairs headquarters in Gatineau; Greg went to the Pearson Building in Ottawa where the department was headquartered. At five o'clock they packed away their files, went to their respective bus stops, and returned home in time for the six o'clock CBC Radio news. Greg then read the newspapers while Brenda prepared dinner. After dinner Greg watched TV until the end of the CBC's eleven o'clock national news program by which time Brenda had returned from a social or business event with friends or colleagues. They then went to bed but didn't have sex. Greg got his from sex workers and Brenda did without. By this time, having children and raising a family together, Brenda's dream when she first met Greg, was out of the question. Greg stayed with her because she was a good house-keeper and he was too lazy to get a divorce. Brenda wanted to leave him but was irrationally afraid he would track her down and force her to come back. Days blended into one another with formless regularity. That was all Greg could look forward to until he retired. That and ostracism and mortgage payments.

The years went by slowly, and Greg's mid-life crisis began. He was only in his forties when his hair turned prematurely white, a bald spot appeared on his crown, and he acquired a turkey neck and the beginnings of a paunch. He was afraid of dying, of time rushing by, and of the absence of meaning in his life. His thoughts turned to India and the way the Hindus prepared for death in that ancient country. At his age they were already looking back on their lives, celebrating the good and atoning for the bad in preparation for the departure of their souls. If the bad outweighed the good, their souls returned as members of a lower caste … or as animals or insects. If the good outweighed the bad, their souls returned as members of a higher caste. Greg believed that made more sense than Judaism, Christianity, or Islam where the good went to heaven and the sin-ful to hell.

Like Nietzsche, Greg no longer believed in God, heaven, and hell. Like Dostoyevsky's Ivan Karamazov, he now assumed that in the absence of God all things were permitted, such as killing an Indian girl at the Desolation River. The Beatitudes now had no meaning. His conscience no longer troubled him. He thought back to his life in Barrie before he'd caught the Greyhound to Murdoch, to his innocence, to his adolescent search for the meaning of life, and to his expectation that he was destined to do great things before he died. He thought of his precocious interest in the Divine, the Big Bang, quantum mechanics, time, space, Tolstoy, Joyce, T.S. Eliot, Beethoven, Schubert, Verdi, Wagner, and Bartók. The spark had been extinguished with the death of the Indian girl, and Greg wanted it back.

Meanwhile, he spent hours at work or alone at home when Brenda was out working or visiting friends brooding about lost opportunities. He now regretted turning down Raúl's offer to become an informant working for MININT out of Ottawa. So what if the RCMP caught him and he went to jail! Anything was better than a slow death from boredom working in Historical Division. He wanted to relive the excitement of his days in Havana when he had slept with the most exciting courtesan in town and spied on Canada for MININT. He would go to Cuba to see if Raúl was still working for MININT and prepared to renew his offer.

12

RETURN TO CUBA

VARADERO, CUBA, JULY 2016

Fourteen years after leaving Cuba, Greg and Brenda went back, this time as tourists carrying ordinary passports on a package tour. At Varadero's airport their charter flight joined a line of Iberia, Mexicana, Delta, and American Airlines aircraft creeping along an access runway leading to the terminal. Tourism had boomed in the years they'd been away, with more than a million Canadians, not counting Mexicans, Brazilians, Argentines, Spaniards, French, Germans, Italians, and Russians, as well as growing numbers of Americans pouring into the country each year. In the old days, visitors had to accept monotonous meals of chicken, black beans, rice, fried bananas, yucca, and plantains, as well as leaky faucets, toilets without seats, toilets without toilet paper, bugs, bad service, and broken-down air conditioners because the prices were dirt cheap. In 2016 the services were supposed to be better, but prices were higher.

It took an hour for buses to come take the passengers from the aircraft to the terminal building, but Greg didn't care. He smelled the sea of Cuba again, and that brought back memories of Neurka and his meetings with her on the beach. Eventually, they reached the arrivals section where men, women, and children came together in a traffic jam before reaching the immigration counter. When it was Greg's turn to show his passport, he passed a note to the official on duty addressed to Raúl Cárdenas, saying Raúl was an old friend and he wanted to see him urgently if the man was still working for MININT. The official took down the name of Greg's hotel and undertook to pass on the message to his superiors to deal with.

Then it was a race against the other passengers to find a baggage cart and elbow their way through the crowd to pick up their luggage from the carousel. It was easy to pick out the Cuban-Americans by their Cuban accents, overloaded suitcases, and rope-wrapped carry-on packages — like old photographs of immigrants arriving at Toronto's Union Station from Eastern Europe at the turn of the twentieth century.

A forty-five-minute ride in a tourist bus to the hotel listening to the mindless patter of the smiling tour guide describing the things to see and do in Varadero followed. The guide stood at the door with his hand out as everyone got off and thanked Greg profusely when he gave him an American dollar bill. The staff at the hotel, dressed as Cuban peasants, greeted the guests with frozen smiles, offering them drinks of rum and Coke, hurriedly downed by everyone except the babies and the elderly. The smiling guide told Greg the Canadian guests would stagger around drunk, singing, hooting, making fools of themselves, and bothering people for the duration of their vacations.

Greg remembered a visit he'd once made when he was on posting to Havana escorting a group of Canadian farmers around a giant Cuban collective farm. They'd seen immense herds of cattle, more than fifty thousand, if his memory was correct. The Cubans were defying their tropical climate to raise cool-weather Holstein milk cows in air-conditioned barns, feeding them the best hay and imported grains to increase milk output. The highest producers were featured in the press as Heroes of the Cuban Revolution. State veterinarians had stood by to meet their every need. Greg thought the tourists of today were the new Holsteins, pampered to get the most out of them. He could hardly wait to get to his room.

Three hours later Raúl Cárdenas knocked on Greg's hotel door. The man had put on weight but otherwise looked the same. After some preliminary chit-chat, during which Raúl confirmed he still worked for MININT, he invited Greg and Brenda to join him for a drink at the bar "for old times' sake." Brenda said no, but Greg, of course, accepted. Raúl surprisingly asked no questions at the bar about Greg's work in Ottawa, made no reference to his past services as an informant for MININT, and talked about the weather, the illness of Fidel, the rise of ISIS, the American election campaign, the establishment of diplomatic ties between Cuba and the United States, and the arrival of the Cuban-American tourists. After an hour or so, he glanced at his watch and said, "It was good of you to remember me, but I've got to be going. I'm already late for dinner and don't want to upset my wife."

He then stood and handed Greg a card with a telephone number on it. "Enjoy your vacation, and if there's anything I can do for you, I'd be happy to oblige. Maybe my wife and I could take you and your wife to one of the new restaurants that have opened up in recent years. Just give me a call. Anything to make your visit to our country a pleasant one."

"That would be nice, "Greg said, "but I'm really here to formally accept the offer you made to me back in 2002 to work for MININT in Ottawa."

"But I made that offer fourteen years ago," Raúl said, astonished.

"And I'd like to see Neurka again … for old times' sake. We were such good friends. Could you tell her I'm here in Varadero and would like to see her?"

Raúl started to laugh, gave Greg a big *embrazo*, and said, "You always were a joker." He stuck out his hand, and the two men shook on it, both laughing.

Greg stepped back and told Raúl he was dead serious. He wanted to work for MININT again. He was well placed to provide a lot of classified information. "Think about my offer. Don't turn it down out of hand. Let me know before we go back to Canada on July 16."

"You always were a joker," Raúl repeated, then left.

Despite Raúl's lack of interest, Greg was certain he would get an offer before they boarded the plane.

Greg spent the next few days watching two overweight guests in the room next door. He said hello to them from their shared balcony, and they seemed friendly, but he didn't understand their reply. If he had to guess, he would say they were Finns or Latvians, but he wasn't sure. They stretched out on lounge chairs around the pool from early morning until sunset every day like walruses basking in the sun with interruptions only for meals and naps in the early afternoon, and drank enormous quantities of mojitos, rum and Cokes, and cheap Spanish red wine. Waiters hovered about them in the restaurant and around the bar as if they were cows needing the best of feed to produce the best of milk.

Greg couldn't keep his eyes off them, fascinated by their skimpy bathing suits, loud laughter, and uninhibited pleasure. At night he listened to their lovemaking through the open balcony door. Their skin turned a bright red and began to peel. They applied suntan lotion and went back out into the sun. Then, on the third day, around three in the afternoon, Greg was sitting on the balcony reading. It was hot, thirty-five degrees, the building was quiet, not even the sounds of *muchachas* arguing. There was sudden activity next door — shouts, the voice of a woman in distress. Greg walked over and peered in, not with any intention of helping. He was merely curious. The husband was lying motionless, naked, face up, his eyes wide open and staring at the ceiling, and his wife was running naked out the door to the corridor screaming. Greg smiled. Dying while making love was a good way to go.

The room filled with Canadian vacationers who came to argue over what to do and then pound his chest — everyone it seemed was an expert in resuscitation. Greg returned to his room just after a white-coated Cuban doctor arrived to replace the Canadians. He heard the heavy, rhythmic slaps of hands against naked flesh going on in time to jerky sobs coming from the wife. Greg realized they didn't have a defibrillator in this hotel. There was silence followed by the voice of the wife in broken English. "No autopsy, no violation of body, just do what's necessary to send the body home."

The doctor gently answered, *"Sí, señora, no problema, señora, comprendo, señora."*

The body lay there all afternoon, alone except for the weeping wife, until after dark when they came to get him. Greg went downstairs to the bar, ordered a rum and Coke, and thought about the Finn and his *coitus interruptus* death. He wondered if the man had been satisfied with life, whether the Finn had had a bucket list that would never be fulfilled. Had he wanted to visit Jerusalem or the Taj Mahal before he died? Or maybe write a novel or a play? Did he have children back in Helsinki who would mourn his passing? Was there another woman in his life who would be sad? If his ambition had been to die in bed making love to his wife, then his wish had been granted. Greg had one item on his bucket list — starting a new life as an informant for MININT with Neurka by his side, if he could persuade her to join him.

Afterward, Greg asked the *muchacha* who was replacing the sheets if the employees had orders to keep the death of the Finn quiet. She said they kept all deaths secret. Management didn't want to upset the guests — that was why they always removed the bodies late at night out the back way past the garbage bins. Greg wasn't surprised. Business was business, and hotel rooms like cattle stalls had to keep producing to meet their quotas.

Although he hadn't heard back from Raúl, Greg thought the man might have told Neurka he was back in Cuba and she might come looking for him. It was a long shot, but he began walking the beach, hoping she would appear there behind the hotel and invite him to accompany her to a nearby MININT guest house to spend the night, the way she had in the good old days in Havana. Greg didn't know that even if Raúl had asked her to meet Greg, if just for old times' sake, she would have refused. She had retired from her job at MININT a decade before and wouldn't have wanted to jump into bed with a former informant and jeopardize her life as a happily married housewife with a devoted husband and two adult children and several grandchildren.

Night after night Greg searched for Neurka, and night after night he returned disappointed to his room. Eventually, to pass the time, he struck up a conversation with one of the prostitutes lurking behind the hotel and came to an agreement on the terms and conditions of a sexual encounter. But a cop emerged from the bushes and shooed away the girl, warning Greg that he would run him in if he caught him with a hooker again. The cop pretended not to understand when Greg said he had friends in the upper reaches of MININT. Greg wasn't discouraged and continued to prowl the beach night after night in search of Neurka until Brenda assumed he was spending his time with women provided by MININT. She didn't believe him when he told her he hadn't done anything that should alarm her, but she kept on expressing her concern, anxious to keep him out of trouble.

Matters went downhill from there. Brenda indicated, without saying so explicitly, that she thought Greg was lying. He told her to be quiet, slapped her across the face, and said she would get more of the same if she didn't shut up. Brenda, for once, lost her temper and said that if Josh knew, he wouldn't let Greg get away with his abuse. Greg backed off, started to drink heavily, and said that her family were a bunch of losers — her mother a drunk, her father a thug, Josh a nutcase, and Raven a mouthy slut. He said things that crossed the line. He said the world would be a better place without Indians, and something should be done to get rid of them. He started to cry and said he had never forgiven himself for helping another guy kill an Indian girl in northern Manitoba back in 1990, well before he'd met Brenda. He said his actions were inexcusable, but he'd been drunk, young, and didn't know better. The other guy, a Métis bootlegger, was really to blame. The girl would be forty by now if she'd lived. Probably would have had children of her own, maybe even grandchildren. Indians married young, after all. He said he was sorry. He begged Brenda to forgive him.

Brenda lost control and came after him, scratching his face, sinking her teeth into his nose until he screamed in pain, and hitting him anywhere she could until she ran out of wind and stood there panting. Greg laughed at her, and that made Brenda mad all over again, but this time she used her tongue and not her fists. "Go beg forgiveness from the girl's family and not from me," she said. Greg laughed again, and Brenda said, "I'm not your mother and I'm not in the business of counselling murderers." That made Greg furious, as much for her temerity in opposing him as in what she'd said, and he hit her face with the back of his hand.

She ran outside and didn't come back until she thought Greg was asleep. He heard her talking to Josh on the phone and took it from her before she said too much. They began to fight again. But instead of giving up when Greg gained the upper hand, Brenda kneed him in the groin and unleashed a series of blows to his face and upper body that sent him reeling. To fend her off, Greg hit her hard with his fist, too hard, in fact, because her head snapped back, she went limp, and fell heavily to the floor. Greg picked her up and placed her on the bed, put his fingers on the artery in her neck to look for a pulse, but didn't find one.

There was a timid knocking on the door, and a voice asked if everything was all right. When Greg didn't answer, there was the noise of an entry card being inserted in its slot and the door opened to let a security guard come in. He looked at Brenda lying on the bed and asked what was wrong. Greg didn't answer. The guard left and came back with the same doctor who had tried to revive the Finn. He worked on her for fifteen or twenty minutes before he gave up and pronounced her dead. He said he was sorry and sat down to fill out a form and ask a few questions. Greg knew that if he wasn't careful he could end up in jail, so he said, "She had a weak heart, and I guess too much sun and alcohol have provoked a heart attack or stroke?" The doctor gazed at Greg and nodded noncommittally.

"She's an Indian, a Canadian Aboriginal Indian, and Canadian Aboriginal Indians are opposed to any procedure that would defile the body after death, such as an autopsy," Greg added.

The doctor turned his eyes to the blood, scratches, and bite marks on Greg's face and answered, *"Sí, señor, no problema, señor, comprendo, señor."*

"And she would have wanted to be cremated and buried locally. Do you understand?"

"Sí, señor, no problema, señor, comprendo, señor," the doctor repeated.

Greg gave him Raúl's telephone number as a reference. To be doubly sure his wishes would be followed, he gave the hotel manager Raúl's number, as well, and told him Raúl was a member of MININT.

After glancing at Greg's face, the manager said, *"Sí, señor, no problema, señor, comprendo, señor."* But it was as if to say, "Go away, you stupid *gringo*, and don't bother me with your bullshit."

EPILOGUE

Brenda woke up in the Hermanos Ameijeiras Hospital in downtown Havana two weeks later with a splitting headache to see Raven and Josh in her room. After rapidly hugging her sister, Raven ran out to summon a doctor who spoke English.

"You're on the way to recovery from a concussion," he told Brenda after he examined her. "I'd like to keep you in the hospital for a few weeks of observation, after which you should be fit to return to Canada."

"What happened to me?" she asked Raven after the doctor left.

"The police told me you and Greg were arguing and he hit you so hard he thought you were dead. Being the kind of guy he is, he made a run for it, but the police caught him at the airport and hauled him off to jail. He's being charged with attempted murder — that's punishable by a life sentence down here."

Brenda burst into tears, and Raven and Josh crowded around, thinking she was crying for Greg, for the tough prison sentence ahead of him, making excuses for him as she always did after he'd slapped her around. But they cried along with her when she said her tears were tears of happiness — tears of gratitude for finally being able to escape his physical and emotional abuse.

"I've wanted to leave him almost from the start of our marriage but didn't dare because I was terrified about what he would do. Now he's in jail and I've been set free."

Brenda returned to Ottawa in early August to report Greg's confession to the police. They followed up, arresting Hubert Leduc in the fall of 2016 for the murder of Betsy Lalonde, the First Nation girl he and Greg had murdered in the summer of 1990. As for Greg, he was tried and convicted in Cuba of attempted murder and sentenced to twenty years of hard labour. He would be extradited to Canada to stand trial for his role in Betsy's murder as soon as he got out of jail there.

Raven called Brenda a year later to congratulate her on obtaining her divorce from Greg and to say Maria had finally complained to the police about the abuse she had been taking from Isaac all these years. "They charged him with assault and bootlegging, and he's now in the Sudbury jail. She didn't want to hang around Yellow Dog waiting for Isaac to get out and come back to beat her again, and so, like a good daughter I invited her to come live with me in Thunder Bay on condition she join Alcoholics Anonymous and quit drinking."

Four months later Raven telephoned Brenda with what she thought was more good news: Maria was doing well, drying out and wanting to see her older daughter. Brenda said no. There was too much bad blood between them. Then Jean called, saying she had read in the newspaper that Greg was in prison in Cuba and asked if she could pay Brenda a visit to make a new start in their relationship. But Brenda said no to her, as well.

And then, just as she thought she was in control of her life for the first time, Brenda received a newspaper clipping from Gloria Larue, the sister of the murdered Betsy Lalonde:

> *Winnipeg Daily News*, November 23, 2017. When Hubert Leduc, charged with the June 1998 murder of Betsy Lalonde, appeared in court on November 22, the public learned details about the background to the case. Crown Prosecutor Donald Harrison said an individual who identified herself as Brenda Chambers had contacted the Ottawa police in August, 2016, with information that had led to the arrest of Leduc. Chambers informed the police that during a holiday in Cuba in July 2016, her husband, Greg Chambers, had told her in the course of a violent domestic dispute that he and an accomplice had been involved in the murder of an Indian girl in the summer of 1990 near the Calvin mine in northeastern Manitoba. Her husband had subsequently attempted to kill her, as well, but she survived. He has been arrested and tried by the Cuban authorities and sentenced to twenty years of hard labour. A team of RCMP investigators from the Winnipeg headquarters visited Chambers in his Cuban jail and took a full statement. It was decided to extradite him from Cuba to stand trial for the death of Lalonde after and not before he served his Cuban sentence.
>
> The prosecutor added that Greg Chambers told the RCMP team that he had become obsessed with all things Indigenous after becoming involved

in the murder of Betsy Lalonde. He spent some
years trying to pass as a Métis when he wasn't one,
eventually marrying and remaining married for
twenty-one years to a member of the Yellow Dog
First Nation in northern Ontario. Mrs. Chambers,
the prosecutor added, was a senior, highly respected,
and long-standing employee of the Department of
Indigenous and Northern Affairs Canada.

Attached to the clipping was the following letter to Brenda
from Gloria:

Dear Mrs. Chambers,

First of all, I'd like to thank you for coming forward and fingering that homicidal husband of
yours for the death of my beloved sister, Betsy.
I was just a kid of eight or nine, and she must
have been fourteen when she disappeared off
the face of the earth. We were both at residential school and looking forward to the end of
term and going home for the summer to what
was then called the Wolverine Indian Reserve but
what's now called the Wolverine First Nation. In
those days, the kids went to the residential school
a hundred kilometres away and not far from the
Calvin mine. Our only way out was by air or dog
team, but now there's an all-weather road.

School ended about a week after Betsy disappeared. I had gone to the administration to
report her missing, but the teachers were getting
ready for their summer holidays and didn't want

to be bothered. They said Betsy probably got homesick and walked home through the bush. They said she'd be waiting for me on the shore when the float plane ferried the kids home for the summer. I told them Betsy would never run off like that without telling me, but they didn't want to listen.

And, of course, she wasn't there on the shore when I got off the plane. I didn't even have to tell my parents what had happened. When they saw I was alone, they knew what had happened. Because Betsy wasn't the first girl from our community who'd been murdered and gone missing. We all started to cry and went home to cry some more. My parents contacted the police, but they didn't want to be bothered. They told my parents she had either gone to Winnipeg to be a hooker or had been killed by a bear trying to make it home. Other girls from our reserve went missing afterward, and still the police did nothing to catch that serial killer.

And then you appear out of the woodwork with the answer to what happened! I only wish you had come forward when my parents were still alive. They never got over her disappearance. Eventually, they would have been happy just to get confirmation she was dead, for confirmation she wasn't still suffering.

Now I'd like to get something off my chest. Either you knew he killed Betsy and were in cahoots with him, or you knew but were too afraid to tell on him, or you didn't know and that's the reason you didn't speak up. But even if you didn't know, how could you have lived for so long with a monster like that? I bet he used to beat you. That's a good sign of someone who'd kill an Indian woman one day. Did you go to the police and complain? Maybe he'd have confessed if they'd got him alone for a couple of hours of tough questioning. Did he chase women? That's another sign. Didn't you wonder why he tried so hard to be an Indigenous person when he wasn't one? That's a sign of a troubled man. I really don't know what to think. But whatever happened, I don't blame you. Me and the members of my family have closure, but you have to live with your conscience.

— Gloria Larue

RECOMMENDED
BACKGROUND READINGS

I

THE SIXTIES SCOOP

Summary Judgment on the Common Issue
Superior Court of Justice
February 2017

[1] After eight years of protracted procedural litigation, the Sixties Scoop class action is before the court for a decision on the first stage of the merits. The representative plaintiff brings this motion for summary judgment asking that the certified common issue, which focuses on the liability of the federal government, be answered in favour of the class members. If the common issue is answered in favour of the class members, the class action will proceed to the damages stage. If the common issue is answered in favour of the federal government, the class action will be dismissed.

[2] Both sides agree that the common issue can be summarily decided. I do as well. For ease of reference I will refer to the defendant government as "Canada" or "the Federal Crown."

BACKGROUND

[3] The background facts, as set out in the six previous decisions, are by now well known, not only to the parties but to many Canadians, and will not be repeated here. In any event, the factual background is not in dispute.

[4] The Sixties Scoop happened and great harm was done.

[5] There is no dispute about the fact that thousands of Aboriginal children living on reserves in Ontario were apprehended and removed from their families by provincial child welfare authorities over the course of the class period — from 1965 to 1984 — and were placed in non-Aboriginal foster homes or adopted by non-Aboriginal parents.

[6] There is also no dispute about the fact that great harm was done. The "scooped" children lost contact with their families. They lost their Aboriginal language, culture, and identity. Neither the children nor their foster or adoptive parents were given information about the children's Aboriginal heritage or about the various educational and other benefits that they were entitled to receive. The removed children vanished "with scarcely a trace." As a former Chief of the Chippewas Nawash put it: "[i]t was a tragedy. They just disappeared."

[7] The impact on the removed Aboriginal children has been described as "horrendous, destructive, devastating, and tragic." The uncontroverted evidence of the plaintiff's experts is that the loss of their Aboriginal identity left the children fundamentally disoriented, with a reduced ability to lead healthy and fulfilling lives. The loss of Aboriginal identity resulted in psychiatric disorders,

substance abuse, unemployment, violence, and numerous suicides. Some researchers argue that the Sixties Scoop was even "more harmful than the residential schools":

> Residential schools incarcerated children for ten months of the year, but at least the children stayed in an Aboriginal peer group; they always knew their First Nation of origin and who their parents were and they knew that eventually they would be going home. In the foster and adoptive system, Aboriginal children vanished with scarcely a trace, the vast majority of them placed until they were adults in non-Aboriginal homes where their cultural identity and legal Indian status, their knowledge of their own First Nation and even their birth names were erased, often forever.

[8] One province, Manitoba, has issued a formal apology. On June 18, 2015, the premier of Manitoba apologized on behalf of the province for the "historical injustice" of the Sixties Scoop and "the practice of removing First Nation, Métis, and Inuit children from their families and placing them for adoption in non-Indigenous homes, sometimes far from their home community, and for the losses of culture and identity to the children and their families and communities."

[9] All of this, however, is background and is not determinative of the legal issue that is before the court. The court is not being asked to point fingers or lay blame. The court is not being asked to decide whether the Sixties Scoop was the result of a well-intentioned governmental initiative implemented in good faith and informed by the norms and values of the day, or was, as some maintain, state-sanctioned "culture/identity genocide" that was driven by

racial prejudice to "take the savage out of the Indian children." This is a debate that is best left to historians and, perhaps, to truth and reconciliation commissions.

[10] The issue before this court is narrower and more focused. The question is whether Canada can be found liable in law for the class members' loss of Aboriginal identity *after* they were placed in non-Aboriginal foster and adoptive homes.

COMMON ISSUE

[11] The certified common issue that is before the court for adjudication is this:

> When the Federal Crown entered into the *Canada-Ontario Welfare Services Agreement* in December 1, 1965, and at any time thereafter up to December 31, 1984:
>
> (1) Did the Federal Crown have a fiduciary or common law duty of care to take reasonable steps to prevent on-reserve Indian children in Ontario who were placed in the care of non-Aboriginal foster or adoptive parents from losing their Aboriginal identity?
> (2) If so, did the Federal Crown breach such fiduciary or common law duty of care?

[12] Three observations should be made. First, the *Canada-Ontario Welfare Services Agreement* entered into on December 1, 1965 ("the

1965 Agreement" or "the Agreement"), is obviously at the core of the common issue. Second, the focus of the common issue is the action or inaction of Canada, not Ontario; and, three, the focus of attention is only on the time period after the Aboriginal children had been placed in non-Aboriginal foster or adoptive homes. The actual apprehension and removal of the children from the reserves by provincial child-care workers is not an issue that is before the court.

[13] Put simply, the common issue asks whether Canada had and breached any fiduciary or common law duties (when it entered into the 1965 Agreement or over the course of the class period) to take reasonable steps in the post-placement period to prevent the class members' loss of Aboriginal identity.

CLASS DEFINITION

[14] The class is defined to include the estimated 16,000 Aboriginal children who were removed from reserves in Ontario and placed in non-Aboriginal foster homes or were adopted by non-Aboriginal parents. The class period covers nineteen years — from December 1, 1965 (when Canada entered into the 1965 Agreement), to December 31, 1984 (when Ontario amended its child welfare legislation to recognize for the first time that Aboriginality should be a factor to be considered in child protection and placement matters).

THE 1965 AGREEMENT

[15] The genesis of the 1965 Agreement can be found in the discussions that took place at the 1963 Federal-Provincial Conference. According to the preamble in the 1965 Agreement, the 1963

Conference "determined that the principal objective was the provision of provincial services and programs to Indians on the basis that needs in Indian Communities should be met according to standards applicable to other communities." The stated goal of the 1965 Agreement was to "make available to the Indians in the province the full range of provincial welfare programs."

[16] Under s. 2(1) of the 1965 Agreement, Ontario undertook to extend some eighteen provincial welfare programs to "Indians with Reserve Status in the Province." The provincial programs in question, as listed in Schedules A and C to the Agreement, included blind and disabled person allowances, mothers' allowances, care of the aged, and child welfare services, that is "services to children, including the protection and care of neglected children, the protection of children born out of wedlock, and adoption services provided under the [Ontario] *Child Welfare Act* ..."

[17] There is no doubt that Canada could have enacted its own child protection statute aimed only at Indian children on reserves" or, indeed, any of the other seventeen provincial laws that formed part of the 1965 Agreement. But it chose not to do so. Ontario already had operating provincial programs in place. And even though the province could have extended these laws to the reserves as "laws of general application" under s. 88 of the *Indian Act*, it was clearly not doing so. It made sense, therefore, for Canada to fund the provincial extension to the reserves of the eighteen listed provincial laws as an exercise of its spending power. Canada's financial obligation under the 1965 Agreement was to reimburse the province for the per capita cost of the provincial programs that were so extended, in accordance with the formula that was set out in the Agreement.

[18] It is important to understand, however, that the 1965

Agreement was more than a federal spending agreement. It also reflected Canada's concern that the extension of the provincial laws would respect and accommodate the special culture and traditions of the First Nations peoples living on the reserves, including their children.

[19] That is why section 2(2) was added.

OBLIGATION TO CONSULT UNDER SECTION 2(2)

[20] Ontario's undertaking to extend the provincial welfare programs as set out in section 2 (2) was made "subject to (2)." Sub-section 2(2) of the Agreement said this:

> No provincial welfare program shall be extended to any Indian Band in the Province unless that Band has been consulted by Canada or jointly by Canada and by Ontario and has signified its concurrence.

[21] It is obvious not only from the plain meaning of this provision but also from the circumstances surrounding the execution of the 1965 Agreement that the obligation to consult with Indian Bands and secure their concurrence was intended to be a key component of the Agreement. One only has to consider what was said in a background memorandum prepared by Canada for use at the 1963 Federal-Provincial Conference:

> The utmost care must be taken ... to ensure that the Indians are not again presented with a fait accompli in the form of a blueprint for their future which they have had no part in developing and which they

have been given no opportunity to influence. This means that the Federal Government should make crystal clear that before any final arrangements are made, the Indians must be fully consulted.

[22] Consider as well what was said by Mr. Tremblay, the federal Minister of Citizenship and Immigration, in October 1964 to the Federal-Provincial Conference, as summarized in the minutes of the meeting:

> *Consultation with Indians.* Mr. Tremblay, in introducing this topic, said that it is an extremely important one as the success of any federal-provincial effort to extend a provincial service will depend on the Indians accepting the proposal and participating in its development. From past experience, we believe acceptance and co-operation by the Indians will not be secured without adequate consultation with them.

[23] And, in a "circular" dated December 9, 1964, the Assistant Deputy Minister of the Indian Affairs Branch of the federal Department of Citizenship and Immigration advised his federal colleagues that he would view it as a "serious breach of faith with the Indian people if any provincial services were forced on a Band against its wishes":

> It is departmental policy ... to encourage the extension of provincial services to reserves in those areas where Provinces are competent to provide services but under no circumstances must action be taken toward this end — that is

to actually extend a service to a reserve — without the consent of the Indians concerned ...

If an agreement can be arrived at, the next step will be to explain it to each individual Band in the Province and to ascertain whether the Band wishes the provincial service extended to it. If it is unacceptable to any Band, no extension of that particular service will be made to that Band and the service provided by the Federal Government will continue.

It is important that the Indians understand Federal policy in this regard and this circular may be helpful to you in your future discussions with them. *I would consider it to be a serious breach of faith with the Indian people if any provincial services were forced on a Band against its wishes.* [Emphasis added.]

[24] In short, Canada was prepared to exercise its spending power to fund the extension of the provincial programs to reserves but only with the advice and consent of every affected Indian Band to every one of the eighteen provincial programs that were being so extended. It is obvious from the record that the obligation to consult, as set out in s. 2(2) of the 1965 Agreement, was intended to include explanations, discussions, and accommodations. It was meant to be a genuinely meaningful provision.

THE OBLIGATION TO CONSULT APPLIED TO CHILD WELFARE SERVICES

[25] Canada argues that the obligation to consult in section 2(2)

of the 1965 Agreement did not apply to Ontario's extension of its child welfare services to the reserves because some level of child protection services had already been extended to some reserves *before* the 1965 Agreement.

[26] It is true that some provincial programs, such as blind and disabled person allowances, care of the aged, and some child welfare services had already been extended to some of the reserves in Ontario. For example, child welfare services were being provided to some reserves in the late 1950s under private agreements between certain Children's Aid Societies (CAS) and the federal government with the latter providing the funding.

[27] However, as Canada itself made clear at the 1963 Federal-Provincial Conference, the provincial services being provided were at best "piecemeal" and "rudimentary." The level of federal funding was "minimal." The 1963 Federal-Provincial Conference was told that provincial services "needed to be increased several times over to bring them up to provincial standards." Canada explained that from its point of view, "it would be highly desirable to accelerate, enlarge, and broaden the pace and scope [of these piecemeal arrangements] with the objective eventually of negotiating master agreements covering the whole field of welfare … on a province-wide basis."

[28] Hence, the 1965 Agreement. The Agreement extended, among other things, the whole field of "services to children, including the protection and care of neglected children, the protection of children born out of wedlock, and adoption services provided under the *Child Welfare Act*" to Indian reserves, on a province-wide and provincial standards basis. The level of federal funding was now significant as was the impact on the reserves.

[29] If any of the provincial programs proved "unacceptable" to any Band, as was made clear in the federal memorandum of December 9, 1964, discussed above, then "no extension of that particular service will be made to that Band and the service provided by the Federal Government will continue." In other words, absent consultation and acceptance by the individual Band of the provincial child welfare regime, the pre-existing "piecemeal" and "rudimentary" service provided by the federal government (via private contractual agreements with certain CAS organizations in certain parts of the province) would continue.

[30] Canada's submission that the obligation to consult in section 2(2) of the 1965 Agreement did not apply to child welfare services does not succeed. The language in section 2(2) is clear and unambiguous and there is nothing in the discussion papers or other documents surrounding the formation of the 1965 Agreement that suggests in any way that the obligation to consult set out in section 2(2) was not intended to apply to the extension of provincial child welfare services.

[31] Indeed, it strains credulity to think that Canada would repeatedly emphasize the importance of genuine consultation and how it would be "a serious breach of faith" if *any* of the provincial programs were "forced on a Band against its wishes," all the while intending that child welfare services, probably the most intrusive of the provincial programs, could be extended to the reserve without any consultation whatsoever.

[32] In sum, the 1965 Agreement was a watershed event that extended some eighteen provincial welfare programs, including child welfare services, on a province-wide and provincial standards basis to Indians on the reserves. The obligation to consult as set

out in section 2(2) applied plainly and unambiguously to every provincial welfare program, including child welfare services. There was no carve-out for child protection services.

[33] For the balance of my analysis, I will focus on the obligation to consult as it related to the extension of the provincial child welfare regime to the reserves.

NO INDIAN BANDS WERE EVER CONSULTED

[34] The plaintiff says no Indian Bands were ever consulted and the full reach of the provincial child welfare regime was extended to all of the reserves without any consultation and concurrence on the part of any Indian Band.

[35] The plaintiff is right.

[36] On the record before me, I find that no Indian Bands were ever consulted before provincial child welfare services were extended to the reserves and no Bands ever provided their "signified concurrence" following such consultations. The evidence supporting the plaintiff on this point is, frankly, insurmountable. In any event, Canada offered no evidence to suggest otherwise.

CANADA BREACHED THE 1965 AGREEMENT

[37] I find that by failing to consult the Indian Bands, Canada breached section 2(2) of the 1965 Agreement. This finding may seem self-evident but it requires some explanation.

[38] Under section 2(1) of the Agreement, Ontario undertook to extend the listed provincial welfare programs to Indians on reserves but did so "subject to (2)" which required consultation by Canada. One could argue that it was Ontario that breached sections 2(1) and (2) of the Agreement because it proceeded to extend the named provincial programs to the reserves even though Canada had not consulted any Indian Band. The plaintiff, however, filed this class action against Canada, not Ontario.

[39] The question therefore is whether Canada breached section 2(2) of the Agreement. Strictly speaking, there is nothing in section 2(2) which explicitly obliges Canada to actually undertake the consultations referred to therein. However, the undertaking to do so can be implied from the language and context of this provision. The law is clear that a contractual term can be implied if it is a contractual term that must have been intended by the parties and is necessary or obvious in light of the particular circumstances of the agreement. The law is also clear that "where the approval of a third party is necessary in order to enable a contract to proceed, it may be implied that the party in a position to seek that approval must make reasonable efforts to do so."

[40] I therefore have no difficulty concluding that under section 2(2) of the 1965 Agreement, Canada undertook to consult with the Indian Bands, that it failed to do so and thus breached this provision of the Agreement.

IF THE INDIAN BANDS HAD BEEN CONSULTED

[41] Canada argues that even if it had consulted with the Indian bands, as it was obliged to do under section 2(2), there is no

evidence that any of the Indian bands would have provided any ideas or advice that could have prevented the Indian children who had been removed and placed in non-Aboriginal foster or adoptive homes from losing their Aboriginal identity. Counsel for Canada put it this way: "[W]ould life have been different had they been consulted?"

[42] This is an odd and, frankly, insulting submission. Canada appears to be saying that even if the extension of child welfare services to their reserves had been fully explained to the Indian Bands and if each Band had been genuinely consulted about their concerns in this regard, that no meaningful advice or ideas would have been forthcoming.

[43] In the documentation produced by Canada over the course of the class period, there are numerous memoranda and letters from both federal and First Nations representatives setting out in some detail the kinds of things that could have been done to prevent the loss of Aboriginal identity post-placement. For example: educating non-Aboriginal foster and adoptive parents about the relevant cultural differences and providing them with information about the Aboriginal child's entitlement to various federal benefits and payments.

[44] Direct evidence from Indian Band representatives as to what they would have said or advised had they been consulted in 1965 was presented, but in broad brush. Wilmer Nadjiwon, former Chief of the Chippewas Nawash, filed an affidavit that stated if his Indian Band had been consulted he would have "done whatever [he] could" to assist the removed Indian child "to reconnect with his or her family or learn about their First Nations identity." I required more specificity.

[45] I therefore directed a mini-trial under Rule 20.04(2.2) for the purposes of clarification and ordered that the representative plaintiff present oral evidence on the following issue:

> If Canada had consulted with Indian Bands (as per s. 2(2) of the 1965 Agreement) what ideas or advice would have been provided that could have prevented the Indian children who had been removed and placed in non-Aboriginal foster or adoptive homes from losing their Aboriginal identity?

[46] The plaintiff filed two brief affidavits for the mini-trial: one from Wilmer Nadjiwon who had been the Chief of the Chippewas Nawash from 1964 to 1978 and the other from Howard Jones who had been a Band Councillor on the same reserve over some fifteen years beginning in 1965. Upon receiving the affidavits, Canada advised that it not cross-examine and that the two affidavits could stand as the oral testimony. As a result, it was agreed that there was no need for the formal mini-trial.

[47] The uncontroverted evidence of Mr. Nadjiwon and Mr. Jones was that if they had been consulted they would have suggested that some contact be maintained with the removed children during the post-placement period so that they would know that they were loved and "could always come home"; and that the "white care-givers" be provided with information about the removed child's Indian Band, culture, and traditions and the various federal educational and financial benefits that were available to the Indian children.

[48] There is no reason to believe that similar ideas would not have been provided by other Indian Bands had they been consulted and Canada has not adduced any evidence to the contrary.

[49] If these ideas and suggestions had been implemented as part of the extension of the provincial child welfare regime — that is, if the foster or adoptive parents had been provided with information about the Aboriginal child's heritage and the federal benefits and payments that were available when the child became of age, and if the foster or adoptive parents had shared this information with the Aboriginal child that was under their care, it follows in my view that it would have been far less likely that the children of the Sixties Scoop would have suffered a complete loss of their Aboriginal identity.

[50] Canada says things were different back then. Canada argues that in 1965 and in the years immediately following, it was not foreseeable, given the state of social science knowledge at the time, that trans-racial adoptions or placements in non-Aboriginal foster homes would have caused the great harm that resulted.

[51] Canada's submission misses the point.

[52] The issue is not what was known in the 1960s about the harm of trans-racial adoption or the risk of abuse in the foster home. The issue is what was known in the 1960s about the existential importance to the First Nations peoples of protecting and preserving their distinctive cultures and traditions, including their concept of the extended family. There can be no doubt that this was well understood by Canada at the time. For example, focusing on adoption alone, Canada knew or should have known that the adoption of Aboriginal children by non-Aboriginal parents constituted "a serious intrusion into the Indian family relationship" that could "obliterate the [Indian] family and ... destroy [Indian] status."

[53] Recall as well that the Indian Affairs Branch was of the view that "it would be a serious breach of faith with the Indian people

if any provincial services were forced on a Band against its wishes." Indeed, as I have already noted, it was this very understanding, namely the importance to the First Nations peoples of protecting and preserving their distinctive cultures and traditions, that best explains why section 2(2) and the obligation to consult was added to the 1965 Agreement in the first place.

[54] In sum, information about the Aboriginal child's heritage and his or her entitlement to various federal benefits was in and of itself important to both the Indian Band and the removed Aboriginal children — not only to ensure that the latter knew about their Aboriginal roots and "could always come home" but also about the fact that they could apply for the various federal entitlements, including a free university education, and other financial benefits once they reached the age of majority.

[55] Much of this information was finally provided by the federal government in 1980.

THE FEDERAL BOOKLET

[56] Until the publication of the federal informational booklet in or around 1980, Canada had little to no interaction with the removed children or their foster or adoptive parents in the post-placement period. The evidence indicates that on occasion the Indian Affairs Branch of the federal Department of Northern Affairs and National Resources would receive a letter of inquiry from the adoptive parent of a removed Aboriginal child. Here is how the registrar of the Indian Affairs Branch responded on January 7, 1966, to one such letter:

... [*Names redacted*] are registered as Indians. They
have no band number, however, as Indian children
who are adopted by non-Indians are removed from
their natural parents' band number and registered
in a special index so that the facts of their adoption
may be kept confidential. This index also enables
us to identify them as Indians in future if they are
informed of their Indian status and make inquiries
as to their funds, enfranchisement, or other relevant matters. Whether or not they are informed of
their Indian status is left to their adoptive parents.
It is now the policy of the Branch to administer the
funds of children adopted by non-Indians and keep
them available for the children until they become of
age. The funds are held in trust in savings accounts
and paid out to the children on application at any
time after twenty-one years of age.

[57] Three points are made clear in this response: (i) the Indian
Affairs Branch maintained a special registry of adopted Indian
children that would allow them to be identified as Indians in the
future but only "if they are informed of their Indian status and
make inquiries as to their [entitlements]"; (ii) the Indian Affairs
Branch was not providing any such information to the adoptive parents ("whether or not [the children] are informed of their
Indian status is left to their adoptive parents"); and (iii) the Indian
Affairs Branch was holding the monies that were payable to the
adopted children in trust accounts, to be released when they
turned twenty-one and made the required "application."

[58] In short, the only way that an apprehended Aboriginal child
would ever learn about his or her Aboriginal identity or the various

federal entitlements was if he or she had the good fortune to be placed in a home where the non-Aboriginal foster or adoptive parents themselves knew and shared this information with the Aboriginal child or if the child or his non-Aboriginal parents made the effort to obtain this information by writing to the federal government. Canada, however, took no steps to provide any of this information on its own — at least not until 1980.

[59] In or around 1980, the federal department of Indian and Northern Affairs published a detailed informational booklet titled *Adoption and the Indian Child* that was "meant to encourage adoptive parents to inform their adopted Indian children of their heritage and rights." The booklet provided information about the adopted child's Aboriginal heritage and status, the various federal benefits and entitlements that were available, including band payments and treaty annuities. It also explained that the Department was placing these monies into trust accounts and that the child could apply to have these amounts paid out once he or she reached the age of majority. The informational booklet was published in response to "concerns expressed by First Nations individuals and groups that adoptions of Indian children by non-Indian parents would result in the children not learning of their heritage as registered Indians."

[60] Canada's evidence is that the booklets were provided to the province so that CAS workers could distribute them to non-Aboriginal adoptive parents. The plaintiff, however, says there is no evidence that any CAS workers ever received these booklets and certainly no evidence that they were ever distributed to the adoptive parents. In any event, the evidence is clear that Canada took no steps to provide such information until this booklet was published in 1980, some fifteen years after the 1965 Agreement — and then only directed to adoptive parents, not foster parents.

[61] What would have happened if Canada had honoured its obligation to consult the Indian Bands under s. 2(2) of the 1965 Agreement? In all likelihood, as the evidence filed for the mini-trial shows, the Indian Bands would have expressed the same concerns (in 1966) that years later prompted Canada to publish *Adoption and the Indian Child*. If Canada had honoured its obligation to consult the Indian Bands under s. 2(2) of the 1965 Agreement, the information about the child's Aboriginal identity and culture and the available federal benefits would have been provided years sooner and would probably have been provided, via the CAS, to both foster and adoptive parents and not just the latter.

RETURNING TO THE COMMON ISSUE

[62] Let me sum up what I have found thus far. I have found that Canada was obliged under section 2(2) of the 1965 Agreement to consult with each Indian Band before any provincial welfare program, including child welfare services, was extended to the reserve in question. I have found that no such consultations ever took place. I have also found that if the Indian Bands had been consulted they would have suggested, among other things, that information about the apprehended child's Aboriginal heritage and the availability of federal benefits be provided to the foster or adoptive parents. This booklet alone, assuming that the foster and adoptive parents would have shared this information with the Aboriginal child in their care, would probably have prevented the loss of the apprehended child's Aboriginal identity.

[63] That is, Canada failed to take reasonable steps to prevent the loss of Aboriginal identity in the post-placement period by failing, *at a minimum*, to provide to both foster and adoptive parents

(via the CAS) the kind of information that was finally provided in 1980 and thereafter.

[64] Was Canada legally obliged to provide such information? The plaintiff says yes and makes two submissions, one based on fiduciary law and the second based on the common law. For the reasons that follow, I find that Canada's liability cannot be established under fiduciary law but can be established under the common law. I will explain each of these findings in turn.

FIDUCIARY DUTY OF CARE

[65] The law of fiduciary duty as it applies in the Aboriginal context is not in dispute. Although the Federal Crown stands in a fiduciary relationship with Canada's Aboriginal peoples, a fiduciary relationship alone does not necessarily give rise to a fiduciary duty. In the Aboriginal context, a fiduciary duty may be imposed on the Federal Crown in one of two ways.

[66] First, a duty may arise as a result of the Crown's assumption of discretionary control over a specific Aboriginal interest. The interest must be a communal Aboriginal interest in land that is integral to the nature of the Aboriginal community and their relationship to the land and must be predicated on historic use and occupation.

[67] Second, in cases other than ones involving lands of historic use or occupation, a fiduciary duty may arise if three elements are present: (1) an undertaking by the alleged fiduciary to act in the best interests of the alleged beneficiary; (2) a defined person or class of persons vulnerable to a fiduciary's control; and (3) a legal or substantial practical interest of the beneficiary that stands to be

adversely affected by the alleged fiduciary's exercise of discretion or control. The degree of discretionary control must be "equivalent or analogous to direct administration of that interest."

[68] In my view, a fiduciary duty under the first category cannot be established in this case. The Aboriginal interest in question is not an interest in land and the action herein is not being advanced as a communal claim but as a class action seeking individualized redress.

[69] The attempt to establish a fiduciary duty under the second category also does not succeed on the evidence herein. Even if I were to agree with the plaintiff that the first two elements are satisfied — that the obligation to consult was an undertaking to act in the Indian Band's best interests and there existed a vulnerable group, namely children in need or protection — I would still have difficulty with the third element.

[70] I cannot find on the evidence before me that when Canada undertook the obligation to consult under s. 2(2) of the 1965 Agreement that it assumed such a degree of discretionary control over the protection and preservation of Aboriginal identity that it amounted to a "direct administration of that interest." There is no doubt that the obligation to consult was breached and this resulted in great harm but the degree of discretionary control that is required before a fiduciary duty can be imposed is not present on the evidence before the court.

[71] Fiduciary duty has meaning as a legal term and should not be used "as a conclusion to justify a result." I therefore find on the applicable law that a fiduciary duty of care has not been established.

COMMON LAW DUTY OF CARE

[72] A duty of care at common law, however, has been established. In my view, section 2(2) and the obligation to consult creates a common law duty of care and provides a basis in tort for the class members' claims.

[73] The common law duty of care arises out of the fact that the 1965 Agreement is analogous to a third-party beneficiary agreement. Canada undertook the obligation to consult in order to benefit Indian Bands (and by extension, Indians living on the reserves, including children). The Indian Bands are not parties to the Agreement. But a tort duty can be imposed on Canada as a contracting party in these circumstances. As a leading contracts scholar explains:

> There are ... cases in which the tort duty owed to the third party appears to arise directly from the breach of contract. In recent English cases, for example, solicitors have been held liable to prospective beneficiaries for their failure to draw up a will or execute it properly. Such failures would constitute breach of contractual duties owed to their clients that could not be enforced in a contract claim by the prospective beneficiaries because of the third-party beneficiary rule. Their claim in tort, which avoids the third-party beneficiary rule, appears to flow directly from the initial breach of contract.

[74] Similarly, here, the plaintiff's claim in tort (the existence and breach of a common law duty of care) flows directly from the fact

that at the time of entering the 1965 Agreement, Canada assumed and breached the obligation to consult with the third-party Indian Bands. If the circumstances of a solicitor drafting a will for the benefit of a third-party beneficiary is "sufficient to create a special relationship to which the law attaches a duty of care," the same should follow even more where there is not only a unique and pre-existing "special relationship" based on both history and law but a clear obligation to consult the beneficiaries about matters of existential importance.

[75] I pause here to acknowledge that strictly speaking the third-party beneficiaries under the 1965 Agreement were the Indian Bands not the apprehended children — that is, not the class members. It is certainly open to Canada to take the position that the breach of the Agreement and the duty of care that flowed from this breach applied only to the Indian Bands and not to the removed Indian children. I remain confident, however, that such a formalistic argument, fully acceptable in the commercial context, will not be advanced in the First Nations context where notions of good faith, political trust and honourable conduct are meant to be taken seriously, and where Canada's breach of the 1965 Agreement was so flagrant.

[76] If I am wrong in my conclusion that the common law duty of care as alleged herein can be established under existing law as just described, and instead is better understood as a novel claim, I now turn to the analysis that applies when dealing with a novel claim.

[77] The applicable legal approach is the "two stage" analysis known as the *Anns-Cooper* test. The first stage question is whether the facts disclose a relationship of proximity in which failure to take reasonable care might foreseeably cause loss or harm to the plaintiff. If this is established, a *prima facie* duty of care arises and

the analysis proceeds to the second stage, which asks whether there are any residual policy reasons why this *prima facie* duty of care should not be recognized.

[78] In my view, under the first stage of the analysis, a *prima facie* duty of care is established. It is beyond dispute that there is a special and long-standing historical and constitutional relationship between Canada and Aboriginal peoples that has evolved into a unique and important fiduciary relationship.

[79] It is also beyond dispute that given such close and trust-like proximity it was foreseeable that a failure on Canada's part to take reasonable care might cause loss or harm to Aboriginal peoples, including their children. As the Supreme Court noted in *Cooper v. Hobart*, by looking at the "expectations" and "interests involved" the court can evaluate "the closeness of the relationship between the plaintiff and the defendant" and can "determine whether it is just and fair having regard to that relationship to impose a duty of care in law upon the defendant."

[80] Even in the absence of section 2(2) and the obligation to consult, Canadian law, during the time period in question, "accepted" that Canada's care and welfare of the Aboriginal peoples was a "political trust of the highest obligation." And there can be no doubt that the Aboriginal peoples' concern to protect and preserve their Aboriginal identity was and remains an interest of the highest importance. As the Divisional Court put it: "[i]t is difficult to see a specific interest that could be of more importance to Aboriginal peoples than each person's connection to their Aboriginal heritage."

[81] The content of the 1965 Agreement and Canada's clear obligation to consult and secure the signified concurrence of the

affected Indian Band before the child welfare regime was extended
to that reserve reinforces the conclusion that the proximity criter-
ion is easily satisfied on the evidence herein and that it is indeed
just and fair to impose a duty of care upon the defendant. All the
more so when the focus of the extended child welfare regime was a
highly vulnerable group, namely children in need of protection. I
therefore find that a *prima facie* duty of care has been established.

[82] I can now turn to the second stage of the *Anns-Cooper* analysis.
In my view, Canada has not advanced any credible policy consideration that would negate the common law duty of care. Canada says
that imposing a duty on the federal government to provide essential information about Aboriginal identity and federal financial
benefits to the non-Aboriginal foster and adoptive parents would
"penalize Canada for having used its spending power to ensure that
Ontario had the capacity to provide Indian children on reserves in
need of protection with that very protection." In my view, this submission does not succeed. Imposing a duty of care to provide said
information would not have "penalized" anybody. All that would
have happened in this case is that Canada would have provided
the much-needed information in and around 1965 and not fifteen
years later.

[83] I therefore find that a common law duty to take steps to prevent
Aboriginal children who were placed in the care of non-Aboriginal
foster or adoptive parents from losing their Aboriginal identity has
been established.

ANSWERING THE COMMON ISSUE

[84] In my view, the common issue must be answered as follows.

[85] For the reasons set out above, when Canada entered into the 1965 Agreement and over the years of the class period, Canada had a common law duty of care to take reasonable steps to prevent on-reserve Indian children in Ontario, who had been placed in the care of non-Aboriginal foster or adoptive parents, from losing their Aboriginal identity. Canada breached this common law duty of care.

DISPOSITION

[86] The common issue is answered in favour of the plaintiff. Canada is liable in law for breaching a common law duty of care to the class members. This is not an issue that requires a trial.

[87] The class action now moves forward to the damages assessment stage. Counsel should schedule a case conference to discuss next steps.

[88] The plaintiff is entitled to the costs of this summary judgment motion. These costs are likely to be substantial. If the parties cannot agree on the costs, I would be pleased to receive brief written submissions from the plaintiff within fourteen days and from the defendant within fourteen days thereafter. A brief reply from the plaintiff may follow.

[89] Order to go accordingly.

— JUSTICE EDWARD P. BELOBABA

2

STOLEN SISTERS

Excerpts from the landmark Amnesty International report: *A Human Rights Response to Discrimination and Violence Against Indigenous Women in Canada*, October 2004.

INTRODUCTION

Helen Betty Osborne was a nineteen-year-old Cree student from northern Manitoba who dreamed of becoming a teacher. On November 12, 1971, she was abducted by four white men in the town of The Pas and then sexually assaulted and brutally murdered. A provincial inquiry subsequently concluded that Canadian authorities had failed Helen Betty Osborne. The inquiry criticized the sloppy and racially biased police investigation that took more than fifteen years to bring one of the four men to justice. Most disturbingly, the inquiry concluded that police had long been aware of white men sexually preying on Indigenous women and girls in

The Pas but "did not feel that the practice necessitated any particular vigilance."

The murder of Helen Betty Osborne is one of nine case studies presented in this report. These stories of missing and murdered Indigenous women and girls take place in three of the western provinces of Canada over a period of three decades. In some cases, the crimes remain unsolved. In others, the perpetrators have been identified as intimate acquaintances, strangers, or men encountered in the course of desperate efforts to earn a living. In every instance, it is Amnesty International's view that Canadian authorities should have done more to ensure the safety of these women and girls.

This report examines the following factors which, too long neglected, have contributed to a heightened — and unacceptable — risk of violence against Indigenous women in Canadian cities:

- The social and economic marginalization of Indigenous women, along with a history of government policies that have torn apart Indigenous families and communities, have pushed a disproportionate number of Indigenous women into dangerous situations that include extreme poverty, homelessness, and prostitution.
- Despite assurances to the contrary, police in Canada have often failed to provide Indigenous women with an adequate standard of protection.
- The resulting vulnerability of Indigenous women has been exploited by Indigenous and non-Indigenous men to carry out acts of extreme brutality against them.
- These acts of violence may be motivated by racism, or may be carried out in the expectation that societal indifference to the welfare and safety of Indigenous women will allow the perpetrators to escape justice.

These are not new concerns. Indigenous women's organizations, government commissions such as the inquiry into the murder of Helen Betty Osborne and the Royal Commission on Aboriginal Peoples, and United Nations human rights bodies have all called on Canadian officials to address the marginalization of Indigenous women in Canadian society and to ensure that the rights and safety of Indigenous people are respected and upheld by police and courts. Sadly, fundamental measures that could help reduce the risk of violence to Indigenous women remain unimplemented. This is only one example of the way Canadian authorities have failed in their responsibility to protect the rights of Indigenous women in Canada.

Scope, Methods, and Limitations of This Study

This report examines the role of discrimination in acts of violence carried out against Indigenous women in Canadian towns and cities. This discrimination takes the form both of overt cultural prejudice and of implicit or systemic biases in the policies and actions of government officials and agencies, or of society as a whole. This discrimination has played out in policies and practices that have helped put Indigenous women in harm's way and in the failure to provide Indigenous women the protection from violence that is every woman's human right.

Amnesty International acknowledges that there are many similarities between Indigenous women and non-Indigenous women's experiences of violence in Canada. More needs to be done to address violence against all women. This report is part of a larger, international campaign to stop violence against women.

This report focuses specifically on violence against Indigenous women because of indications of the scale of such violence in Canada, because the link between racial discrimination and violence against Indigenous women has not yet been adequately acknowledged or addressed, and because the victims of this violence are all too often forgotten.

Amnesty International reviewed published reports and the findings of inquests and government inquiries, interviewed survivors of violence and the family members of Indigenous women who have been murdered or who have gone missing, and met with key organizations and individuals who have worked on their behalf. Where possible, the researchers also spoke with police investigators or spokespersons.

The individual stories that form the major part of this report are retold with the permission of the families and friends. Many of the families of missing and murdered Indigenous women in Canada were unable to take this step. Some find it too emotionally difficult talk about their loss. Others have had negative experiences with the way their stories have been told by reporters and academics. There are countless stories that remain untold.

This report focuses primarily on cities in the western provinces of Canada where there is a large and growing Indigenous population and where there have been a number of highly publicized incidents of violence against Indigenous women. There were regions of Canada that Amnesty International did not have the opportunity to visit in the course of this research and as a result many specific experiences, such as those of Inuit and other northern Indigenous women, the experiences of rural Indigenous women, and Indigenous women living on reserves, unfortunately are not adequately reflected. As was stated by many interviewees, this report is still only "scratching the surface." However, Amnesty International hopes that it will contribute to a fuller understanding of the issue from a human rights perspective.

Violence against women, and certainly violence against Indigenous women, is rarely understood as a human rights issue.

To the extent that governments, media, and the general public do consider concerns about violence against women, it is more frequent for it to be described as a criminal concern or a social issue. It is both of those things, of course. But it is also very much a human rights issue. Women have the right to be safe and free from violence. Indigenous women have the right to be safe and free from violence. When a woman is targeted for violence because of her gender or because of her Indigenous identity, her fundamental rights have been abused. And when she is not offered an adequate level of protection by state authorities because of her gender or because of her Indigenous identity, those rights have been violated.

I. THE INTERNATIONAL HUMAN RIGHTS FRAMEWORK

This report addresses violence against Indigenous women as a human rights issue. The concept of human rights is based on the recognition of the inherent dignity and worth of every human being. Through ratification of binding international human rights treaties, and the adoption of declarations by multilateral bodies such as the United Nations, governments have committed themselves to ensuring that all people can enjoy certain universal rights and freedoms.

Amnesty International's research demonstrates that violence experienced by Indigenous women gives rise to human rights concerns in two central ways.

First, is the violence itself and the official response to that violence. When Indigenous women are targeted for racist, sexist attacks by private individuals and are not assured the necessary levels of protection in the face of that violence, a range of their fundamental human rights are at stake. This includes the right to life, the right to be protected against torture and ill treatment, the right to security of the person, and the right to both sexual and racial equality. Canada has ratified all of the key human rights treaties that guarantee these fundamental rights....

The cases in this report and other cases of violence against Indigenous women that are already on the public record do not involve allegations of violence by police or other public officials. But that does not mean that the human rights obligations of governments are not engaged.

International law is clear; governments are of course obliged to ensure that their own officials comply with human rights standards. Governments are also obliged, though, to adopt effective measures to guard against private individuals committing acts which result in human rights abuses. Human rights bodies have made it clear that when governments fail to take such steps, often termed the duty of "due diligence," they will be held accountable under international human rights treaties. The Inter-American Court of Human Rights has described the duty of due diligence as follows:

> An illegal act which violates human rights and which is initially not directly imputable to a State (for example, because it is the act of a private person or because the person responsible has not been identified) can lead to international responsibility of the State, not because of the act itself but because of the lack of due diligence to prevent the violation or to respond to it as required by the Convention.

The Court stressed that this duty of "due diligence" means that a state must take reasonable steps to prevent human rights violations, use the means at its disposal to carry out serious investigations, identify those responsible, impose the appropriate punishment, and ensure that the victim receives adequate reparation. The U.N. Human Rights Committee has stressed that the duty in article 2 of the Covenant on Civil and Political Right to "ensure" the rights included in the Covenant requires appropriate measures be taken to prevent and investigate abuses perpetrated by private persons or entities, punish those responsible, and provide reparations to the victims. This concept of due diligence does not in any way lessen the criminal responsibility of those who carry out acts of violence, including murder, against women. However, the concept does underline the inescapable responsibility of state officials to take action.

In her 2003 report to the U.N. Commission on Human Rights, Radhika Coomaraswamy, the first Special Rapporteur on violence against women, clearly described the content of the duty of due diligence when it comes to preventing violence against women.

States must promote and protect the human rights of women and exercise due diligence:

(a) to prevent, investigate, and punish acts of all forms of violence against women, whether in the home, the workplace, the community or society, in custody, or in situations of armed conflict;

(b) to take all measures to empower women and strengthen their economic independence and to protect and promote the full enjoyment of all rights and fundamental freedoms;

(c) to condemn violence against women and not invoke custom, tradition, or practices in the name of religion or culture to avoid their obligations to eliminate such violence;

(d) to intensify efforts to develop and/or utilize legislative, educational, social, and other measures aimed at the prevention of violence, including the dissemination of information, legal literacy campaigns, and the training of legal, judicial, and health personnel;

(e) to enact and, where necessary, reinforce or amend domestic legislation in accordance with international standards, including measures to enhance the protection of victims, and develop and strengthen support services;

(f) to support initiatives undertaken by women's organizations and non-governmental organizations on violence against women and establish and/or strengthen, at the national level, collaborative relationships with relevant NGOs and with public and private sector institutions.

Second, the range of concerns, some historical and some continuing, which Amnesty International's research has shown to be factors that put Indigenous women at heightened risk of experiencing violence also directly engage a number of fundamental human rights provisions. For instance, past policies revoking the legal Indigenous status of Indigenous women who married non-Indigenous men have already been found by the U.N. Human Rights Committee to have violated minority cultural rights under article 2718 of the International Covenant on Civil and Political Rights. Certainly, the decades-long residential schools program raises a range of human rights concerns related to the physical, sexual, and psychological abuse and ill treatment of the children sent to the schools, but also such economic, social, and cultural rights as the right to education.

The U.N. Committee on Economic, Social, and Cultural Rights has highlighted that the economic marginalization of Indigenous peoples in Canada is of concern with respect to

Canada's obligations under the Covenant on Economic, Social, and Cultural Rights:

> The Committee is greatly concerned at the gross disparity between Aboriginal people and the majority of Canadians with respect to the enjoyment of Covenant rights. There has been little or no progress in the alleviation of social and economic deprivation among Aboriginal people. In particular, the Committee is deeply concerned at the shortage of adequate housing, the endemic mass unemployment, and the high rate of suicide, especially among youth, in the Aboriginal communities. Another concern is the failure to provide safe and adequate drinking water to Aboriginal communities on reserves. The delegation of the State Party conceded that almost a quarter of Aboriginal household dwellings required major repairs and lacked basic amenities.

These concerns engage a number of internationally protected human rights, including the rights to housing, work, health, and an adequate standard of living.

This report highlights some past and present concerns with respect to Indigenous children, such as residential schools and child protection policies as well as some cases involving violence against Indigenous girls. International human rights laws and standards recognize that children need and deserve special protection to ensure the full realization of their potential. The almost universally ratified U.N. Convention on the Rights of the Child establishes as an overarching principle that "in all actions concerning children … the best interests of the child shall be a primary consideration."

The Convention recognizes that there are instances where, in the best interests of the child, children must be removed from an abusive family situation. However, the Convention asserts that, in general, parents or legal guardians have the primary responsibility for ensuring the welfare of their children and should be supported by the state in meeting this responsibility. Notably, the Convention also recognizes that every child has a right to preserve his or her cultural identity and family relations and that Indigenous children, in particular, "shall not be denied the right ... to enjoy his or her own culture, to profess and practice his or her own religion, to use his or her own language."

At the heart of the various human rights concerns documented in this report is discrimination. Amnesty International's research has found that Indigenous women in Canada face discrimination because of their gender and because of their Indigenous identity. The research highlights that this is compounded by further discriminatory treatment that women face due to poverty, ill health, or involvement in the sex trade. Human rights experts have drawn attention to the interconnections between various forms of discrimination and patterns of violence against women. Amnesty International's research has been conducted within a framework that recognizes the intersections between various forms of discrimination, and supports these findings.

In addition to these existing legal obligations, new and emerging international instruments, such as the United Nations' draft *Declaration on the Rights of Indigenous Peoples*, seek to clarify the specific measures needed to ensure the protection and fulfillment of the rights of Indigenous peoples.

II. UNDERSTANDING VIOLENCE AGAINST INDIGENOUS WOMEN

Stolen Generations:
Colonization and Violence Against Indigenous Women

The U.N. Declaration on Violence Against Women calls violence against women "a manifestation of historically unequal power relations between women and men" and a means by which this inequality is maintained." Around the world, inequality between men and women in terms of wealth, social status, and access to power has created barriers to women seeking protection of their rights. These barriers include economic dependence on abusive spouses, fear of having their children taken away if they report the abuse, or knowing that they will not be taken seriously by the police and courts.

Moreover, both the perpetrators of violence against women and those who administer the criminal justice system — judges, prosecutors, police — often hold the pervasive view that women are responsible for violence committed against them or that they deserve to be punished for non-conforming behaviour. So even when a woman does overcome these barriers and report that she has been the victim of a violent attack, she may well meet with an unsympathetic or skeptical response. In the few cases in which a suspect is identified and brought to trial, cases of violence against women often founder unless there is clear and unavoidable evidence of force, illustrating to all that the victim "fought back." The perpetrators of violence against women can thus commit their crimes safe in the knowledge that they will not face arrest, prosecution, or punishment. Impunity for violence against women contributes to a climate where such acts are seen as normal and acceptable rather than criminal, and where women do not seek justice because they know they will not get it.

For Indigenous women in Canada, violence often takes place in a context shaped, in the words of Canada's Royal Commission on Aboriginal Peoples (RCAP), by the power that the dominant society has wielded "over every aspect of their lives, from the way they are educated and the way they can earn a living to the way they are governed." Historically, in most of the Indigenous cultures that are now part of Canada, there were distinct gender roles for women and men but relative equality between them. Through policies imposed without their consent, Indigenous peoples in Canada "have had to deal with dispossession of their traditional territories, disassociation with their traditional roles and responsibilities, disassociation with participation in political and social decisions in their communities, disassociation of their culture and tradition." Colonialism, which has had a profoundly negative impact on Indigenous communities as a whole, has also affected the relations between Indigenous women and Indigenous men, and pushed many Indigenous women to the margins of their own cultures and Canadian society as a whole.

While it is beyond the scope of this report to look at all the ways government policies have impacted on Indigenous women, two historic policies — the dispossession of Indigenous women who married outside their communities and the removal of children to be educated in residential schools — need to be examined because of their profound and lasting impact on social strife within Indigenous communities and on the marginalization of Indigenous women within Canadian society.

RCAP described the legislation governing Indigenous peoples in Canada as being "conceived and implemented in part as an overt attack on Indian nationhood and individual identity, a conscious and sustained attempt by non-Aboriginal missionaries, politicians, and bureaucrats — albeit at times well intentioned — to impose rules to determine who is and is not 'Indian.'" The first of these laws, passed in 1857, allowed Indigenous men to renounce their Indigenous status and the right to live on reserve lands in order to assimilate into non-Indigenous society. Women were not given the same choice: women's status would be determined by the choices made by her husband or father. A second law passed in 1869 stripped women of their Indigenous status and their place in their community if they married a man from another community, even if he was also Indigenous. In addition, children born to an Indigenous woman who married a non-Indigenous man would also be denied status. These laws remained in place for more than a century. Finally, in 1985, after a long struggle by Indigenous women, which included bringing a successful complaint to the U.N. Human Rights Committee, the policies were repealed for being incompatible with protections against discrimination in the new Canadian Charter of Rights and Freedoms.

Over the next decade, more than 130,000 people — mostly women — applied to have their rights and status restored. For the tens of thousands of women who had been affected over the previous century, losing their status meant the loss of independent standing in their community and increased dependence on their spouses. In many cases, the laws led to women losing all ties to their home communities.

During the same period that so many Indigenous women were being uprooted, the federal government was removing large numbers of Indigenous children from their families and communities to attend schools in predominantly non-Indigenous communities. The explicit purpose of providing education outside of the community was to foster assimilation of Indigenous children into European Canadian culture. The first residential schools were opened in the mid-1870s. In the words of the architect of the system, Canadian Member of Parliament Nicholas Flood Davin, the goal was to remove Indigenous children from "the influence of the wigwam" and keep them instead "constantly within the circle of civilized conditions." The children attending residential schools were not allowed to speak their Indigenous languages or to practise their own customs, eroding their sense of identity and driving a wedge between the children and their parents.

Initially, the schools offered low-quality education geared to industrial trades for boys and domestic service for women. Beginning in the mid-twentieth century, they gradually became residences for Indigenous children attending schools in predominantly non-Indigenous communities. The school system was run in collaboration with Christian churches until 1969. Then, in a phase-out period that lasted through the mid-1980s, the system was run solely by the federal government.

Many children in the schools faced inhuman living conditions caused by chronic underfunding and neglect. Harsh punishments sanctioned by the school authorities included beatings, chaining children to their beds, or denying them food. Cloaked by society's indifference to the fate of these children, individual staff carried out horrendous acts of physical and sexual abuse. Summarizing the history of the residential school system, the RCAP points out "head office, regional, school, and church files are replete, from early in the system's history, with incidents that violated the norms of the day." Yet even the most alarming reports of abuse and neglect were largely ignored by the church and government officials responsible for the care of these children.

> The avalanche of reports on the condition of children "hungry, malnourished, ill-clothed, dying of tuberculosis, overworked" failed to move either the churches or successive governments "to concerted and effective remedial action." When senior officials in the department and the churches

became aware of cases of abuse, they failed routinely to come to the rescue of children they had
removed from their real parents.

In a climate of total impunity, staff carried out their crimes
without fear of repercussion. However, the consequences for many
of the children exposed to repeated abuse stayed with them their
whole lives and have impacted subsequent generations. Like other
survivors of abuse, many of the residential school alumni have carried a sense of shame and self-loathing. Perhaps most harmfully,
they were denied the opportunity to be exposed to good examples
of parenting and instead learned violence and abuse.

With the end of the residential school system, survivors began to
come forward to tell stories of abuse and demand justice. In the early
1990s, there were a number of prosecutions of staff who had abused
children. Following the 1996 RCAP report, the federal government
established a $350 million fund to provide healing programs for
the victims and their families. Applications for support, however,
have greatly outstripped the available resources. Indigenous peoples'
organizations also argue that there has been inadequate redress for
the loss of culture and identity and the intergenerational impacts
of all the forms of abuse suffered in the schools. Although the federal government has apologized for the harm done by the residential
school system, it has failed to act on RCAP's recommendation that
a public inquiry be held so that the injuries suffered by Indigenous
communities can be fully acknowledged.

Indigenous peoples' organizations have pointed out that the
erosion of cultural identity and the accompanying loss of self-worth
brought about, in part, through assimilationist policies like residential schools and the arbitrary denial of some women's Indigenous
status have played a central role in the social strife now faced by many
Indigenous families and communities. In the course of researching

this report, Amnesty International heard from many families who described the personal loss and hardship they have experienced as a consequence of these policies. Some described losing all contact with a sister or daughter who simply disappeared after being put into a foster home or marrying a man from another community. Other women described increasing desperate and dangerous lives shaped by loss of culture, community, and self-esteem. These are two examples of the stories we have heard:

- Margaret Evonne Guylee's mother was from the Whitedog Reserve in Northern Ontario but had been forced to give up her residence in the community in the early 1930s after getting involved with a non-Indigenous man. Margaret Guylee grew up in poverty in Toronto. She then raised six children herself while living on social assistance. She disappeared in 1965. No missing persons report was ever filed. Her daughter, Carrie Neilson, who was only four when her mother disappeared, says she still carries the pain and bewilderment caused by her mother's sudden and still unexplained disappearance. "We believed for years that we were not any good — after all, why would a mother abandon her children if they were good?"

- Edna Brass is a respected elder and counsellor working with Indigenous women in Vancouver. As a child, Edna Brass spent thirteen years in residential school. She remembers being teased by the other children about a cleft palate that left scars on her face. She remembers worse abuse at the hands of the staff running the school: "I was sexually abused, I was raped, I was beaten." As a consequence of what she endured, Edna Brass says she lost her ties to her culture and lost her own way in life. She entered into a life of substance abuse and living on the streets. Although she was eventually able to pull her own life together, she says her family still suffers the scars of her own uprooting. Edna Brass says, "I, myself, didn't have a home. I felt like I didn't belong anywhere and my children have felt the same. They don't know my family. They don't know my community. I never felt like my reserve is my reserve. I just try to fit in where I can. My daughter suffered because of this."

These personal accounts illustrate one of the central conclusions of the Royal Commission on Aboriginal Peoples. "Repeated assaults on the culture and collective identity of Aboriginal people have weakened the foundations of Aboriginal society and contributed to the alienation that drives some to self-destruction and anti-social behaviour," RCAP concluded. "Social problems among Aboriginal people are, in large measure, a legacy of history.

It is important to emphasize that the disruption of Indigenous families and communities is not a thing of the past. Even as the residential school system was being transformed and eventually phased out from the late 1950s through the 1970s, provincial and territorial governments began to place a dramatically increased number of Indigenous children in foster homes and state institutions. One study found that the number of Indigenous children in state care in the province of British Columbia rose from twenty-nine children in 1955 to 1,446 in 1965. Despite many changes that have taken place in the field of Indigenous child welfare, the Canadian government recently estimated that Indigenous children are currently four to six times more likely than non-Indigenous children to be removed from their families and placed in the care of the state.

These children are being removed from their families and communities to protect them from abuse and neglect. There are clearly circumstances where such measures are needed to protect the rights and welfare of the child. Unlike the residential school system, child welfare institutions are not intending to break children's ties to their families and communities. In fact, since the early 1980s, child services in Indigenous communities are increasingly provided by Indigenous organizations funded by the federal government. However, many Indigenous peoples' organizations and other commentators have noted that Indigenous children are often removed from families who want to care for them, but for reasons such as poverty, substance addiction, and other legacies of past government policies are unable to do so. And they question why there are not more resources available to help Indigenous families address situations of impoverishment, stress, and poor parenting before they reach the point where children are endangered.

A joint study completed in 2000 by the Department of Indian Affairs and Northern Development and Assembly of First Nations found that on average Indigenous-run child services programs receive 22 percent less funding than provincially funded counterparts serving predominantly non-Indigenous communities. The study also found that there was not enough emphasis on funding early intervention programs so that children's welfare and safety could be assured without removal from their families.

"You put a child into care and they get counselling immediately," one witness told a parliamentary committee, "but when a biological parent is looking for those sources or that funding to maintain their own family and keep it together, it's not available to them."

The painful loss of ties to family, community, and culture is a common element of many of the stories of missing and murdered women that have been reported to Amnesty International, some of which are presented in the case studies that follow below. Such loss is not a necessary consequence of children being removed from their families, or even of being adopted into a non-Indigenous family. Some of these women were clearly raised with love and affection by caring foster or adoptive families. There are many ways that ties to their heritage and identity could have been maintained throughout their childhood or, if they had had the chance, rebuilt in later life. Nor is loss of culture a direct cause of violence. However, for young people in particular, a loss of a sense of identity, belonging, and ultimately self-worth needs to be understood and addressed as a critical factor potentially contributing to self-destructive behaviour and in vulnerability to exploitation by others.

Indigenous Women in Canadian Cities:
Displaced in Their Own Land

The Canadian government's Royal Commission on Aboriginal Peoples acknowledged in its 1996 report that there have been widespread violations of Indigenous peoples' land and resource rights — including the erosion of more than two-thirds of the land base of Indigenous communities — since the formation of the Canadian state. The Commission warned:

> Without adequate lands and resources, Aboriginal nations will be unable to build their communities and structure the employment opportunities necessary to achieve self-sufficiency. Currently on the margins of Canadian society, they will be pushed to the edge of economic, cultural, and political extinction. The government must act forcefully, generously, and swiftly to assure

the economic, cultural, and political survival of
Aboriginal nations.

With the loss of traditional livelihoods within Indigenous
communities, the opportunities for education and employment
in Canadian towns and cities have become a powerful draw for
a growing number of Indigenous people. Almost 60 percent of
Indigenous people in Canada now live in urban settings. Critically,
however, the majority of Indigenous peoples in Canadian
towns and cities continue to live at a disadvantage compared to
non-Indigenous people, facing dramatically lower incomes and a
shortage of culturally appropriate support services in a government
structure that has still not fully adjusted to the growing urban
Indigenous population.

In the 1996 census, Indigenous women with status living
off-reserve earned on average $13,870 a year. This is about $5,500
less than non-Indigenous women. Other groups of Indigenous
women, such as Inuit and Métis women, recorded slightly higher
average annual incomes, but all substantially less than what
Statistics Canada estimated someone living in a large Canadian city
would require to meet their own needs. In fact, many Indigenous
women living in poverty not only have to look after themselves
but also must care for elderly parents, raise children, or tend to
loved ones in ill health, often with only a single income to live on.
Homelessness and inadequate shelter are believed to be widespread
problems facing Indigenous families in all settings.

The difficult struggle to get by is compounded by many
Indigenous peoples' experience of racism, both subtle and overt,
within the dominant society. As described by the Canadian Panel
on Violence Against Women, "most Aboriginal people have known
racism first-hand — most have been called 'dirty Indians' in
schools or foster homes or by police and prison guards. Aboriginal

people have also experienced subtle shifts in treatment and know it is no accident."

As a whole, Indigenous people living off-reserve move frequently, more so than other people living in Canada. For some, this is movement to and from their home communities as they try to maintain a connection with their families and cultures. For others, this movement may be a reflection of a kind of rootlessness stemming from the fact that their ties to family and community were severed long ago, perhaps by their loss of membership in their home community or perhaps due to their removal to a residential school or some other form of state care. One consequence of this "churn factor," as it is sometimes called, is that many Indigenous people are not aware of — or are unable to access — the services available to them where they live.

In Canada, the federal government is responsible for health and social services on reserve and in Inuit communities, while the provincial and territorial governments provide services elsewhere. This has led to a gap in services for Indigenous people living in Canadian towns and cities. While Indigenous people living off-reserve have access to programs and services designed for the general population, these programs and services are not necessarily aligned to the specific needs of Indigenous peoples, or delivered in a culturally appropriate way....

Indigenous people have formed a wide range of service organizations to help address the needs of the growing urban Indigenous population, including employment counselling, addiction services, health centres, and shelters for women and girls escaping violence. However, most, if not all, report that their work is jeopardized by chronic underfunding and the failure of government to provide funding on a stable, multi-year basis. Being dependent on short-term funding diverts energy from vital services to fundraising, or to managing crises when funds don't arrive. Without stable funding, long-term projects are difficult to plan and organizations fear they won't be able to keep their commitments to the people they serve.

In 2000, the Ontario Federation of Indian Friendship Centres — organizations that represent and provide support to Indigenous people outside their own communities — surveyed Indigenous families about their lives in Ontario cities. All those interviewed described the psychological hardship of their struggle to provide for themselves with little support from the larger community. "Words such as low self-esteem, depression, anger, self-doubt, intimidation, frustration, shame, and hopelessness were used to describe some of the crushing feelings of Aboriginal children and parents living in poverty. Families are feeling despair as they cannot see any way to 'rise above' their situations."

Prostitution is one means that some Indigenous women have resorted to in the struggle to provide for themselves and their families in Canadian cities. A survey of 183 women in the Vancouver sex trade carried out by the PACE (Prostitution Alternatives Counseling and Education) Society found roughly 40 percent of the women said they got into the sex trade primarily because they needed the money, and an additional 25 percent referred to drug addiction as part of the reason they started selling sexual services, while many others referred to pressure from boyfriends or family members. Almost 60 percent said they continued working in the sex trade to maintain a drug habit. In the PACE study, more than 30 percent of sex workers surveyed were Indigenous women, although Indigenous people make up less than 2 percent of the city's population. Indigenous women are believed to be similarly overrepresented among sex workers in other Canadian cities.

The U.N. Committee on the Rights of the Child has expressed concern about "Aboriginal children [in Canada] who, in disproportionate numbers, end up in the sex trade as a means of survival." The non-governmental organization Save the Children Canada spoke with more than 150 Indigenous youths and children being exploited in the sex trade. According to their report, almost all the youth and children interviewed described "the overwhelming presence of disruption and discord in their lives accompanied by low self-esteem." Other factors common to many of the young people's lives included a history of physical or sexual abuse, a history of running away from families or foster homes, lack of strong ties to family and community, homelessness or transience, lack of opportunities, and poverty. The report comments:

> Any trauma that detaches children from their families, communities, and cultures increases the likelihood of involvement in commercial sexual exploitation. Once a child or youth loses such basic parameters as safety, shelter, and sustenance, their vulnerability forces them into situations whereby the sex trade can become the only viable alternative for survival.

III. VIOLENCE AGAINST INDIGENOUS WOMEN: WIDESPREAD BUT POORLY UNDERSTOOD

According to a 1996 Canadian government statistic, Indigenous women between the ages of twenty-five and forty-four with status under the federal *Indian Act* are five times more likely than other women of the same age to die as the result of violence. Indigenous women's organizations have long spoken out against violence against women and children within Indigenous communities — concerns that have still not received the attention they deserve. More recently, a number of advocacy organizations, including the Native Women's Association of Canada (NWAC), have drawn attention to acts of violence perpetuated against Indigenous women in predominantly non-Indigenous communities....

Unfortunately, while there is clear evidence that Indigenous women in Canada face an extraordinarily high risk of violence, significant gaps in how police record and share information about missing persons and violent crimes means that there is no comprehensive picture of the actual scale of violence against Indigenous women, of who the perpetrators are, or in what circumstances the violence takes place. Reports of violent crimes or missing persons may be investigated by municipal police forces, provincial forces, Indigenous police forces, or the national police force, the Royal Canadian Mounted Police (RCMP). Police have said that they do not necessarily record the ethnicity of crime victims or missing persons when entering information into the Canadian Police Information Centre database, the principle mechanism for sharing information among police forces in Canada....

Violence Against Women in the Sex Trade

Whether or not prostitution is a criminal act, women in the sex trade are entitled to the protection of their human rights. Concrete and effective measures must be adopted to ensure their safety and to bring to justice those who commit or profit from violence against sex trade workers.

Working in the sex trade in Canada can be extremely dangerous for women, whether Indigenous or non-Indigenous. This is especially true for women who solicit on the streets. In the PACE study, one-third of the women said they had survived an attack on their life while working on the street.

Women in the sex trade are at heightened risk of violence because of the circumstances in which they work, and because the social stigmatization of women in the sex trade provides a convenient rationale for men looking for targets for acts of misogynistic violence.

There are additional concerns around police treatment of Indigenous and non-Indigenous women in the sex trade. The threat of arrest makes many women reluctant to report attacks to the police or co-operate with police investigations. As a result, the perpetrators may be encouraged by the belief that they are likely to get away with their crimes....

The executive director of Regina's Sex Workers' Advocacy Project, Barb Lawrence, told Amnesty International about comments made by one police officer. A sex worker missed an appointment with a Crown Prosecutor to give testimony in the case of a murdered Indigenous woman in Regina. Lawrence, who had set up the meeting, eventually received a call from the sex worker. It turned out that the woman was being held by city police who wanted her to provide evidence on a separate case. The police had refused to believe that she had a meeting with the prosecutor's office. When Lawrence and the prosecutors went to the police station to meet the woman, the arresting officer reportedly said he had no reason to believe the woman's claims, saying "she's just a hooker on the street."

The isolation and social marginalization that increases the risk of violence faced by women in the sex trade is often particularly acute for Indigenous women. The role of racism and sexism in compounding the threat to Indigenous women in the sex trade was starkly noted by Justice David Wright in the 1996 trial of John Martin Crawford for the murder of three Indigenous women in Saskatchewan:

> It seems Mr. Crawford was attracted to his victims
> for four reasons; one, they were young; second,
> they were women; third, they were Native; and

fourth, they were prostitutes. They were persons separated from the community and their families. The accused treated them with contempt, brutality; he terrorized them and ultimately, he killed them. He seemed determined to destroy every vestige of their humanity.

Racist Violence and Indigenous Women

The Manitoba Justice Inquiry said of the murder of Helen Betty Osborne:

> Her attackers seemed to be operating on the assumption that Aboriginal women were promiscuous and open to enticement through alcohol or violence. It is evident that the men who abducted Osborne believed that young Aboriginal women were objects with no human value beyond sexual gratification.

As the inquiry recognized, racism and sexism intersect in stereotypes of Indigenous women as sexually "available" to men. This intersection of sexism and racism contributes to the assumption on the part of perpetrators of violence against Indigenous women that their actions are justifiable or condoned by society....

Police, however, are inconsistent in their acknowledgement of this threat. Some police spokespersons told Amnesty International that they believe that "lifestyle" factors, such as engaging in the sex trade or illegal drug use, are the most important risk factors, and that other factors such as race or gender are not significant enough to be considered in their work. Other police spokespersons told

Amnesty International that they have seen that racism and sexism are factors in attacks on Indigenous women and that they consider Indigenous women as a whole to be at risk.

Over-Policed and Under-Protected

Numerous studies of policing in Canada have concluded that Indigenous people as a whole are not getting the protection they deserve. This conclusion is supported by the testimony of many of the families interviewed by Amnesty International. A few described police officers who were polite and efficient and who, in a few cases, even went to extraordinary lengths to investigate the disappearance of their loved ones. Other families described how police failed to act promptly when their sisters or daughters went missing, treated the family disrespectfully, or kept the family in the dark about how the investigation — if any — was proceeding.

A number of police officers interviewed by Amnesty International insisted that they handle all cases the same and do not treat anyone differently because they are Indigenous. However, if police are to provide Indigenous people with a standard of protection equivalent to that provided to other sectors of society, they need to understand the specific needs of Indigenous communities, be able to communicate with Indigenous people without barriers of fear and mistrust, and ultimately be accountable to Indigenous communities. As some police officers acknowledged to Amnesty International, this is clearly not the case today.

Across the country, Indigenous people face arrest and criminal prosecution in numbers far out of proportion to the size of the Indigenous population. The Manitoba Justice Inquiry suggested that the overrepresentation of Indigenous people in the justice system may partly stem from the predisposition of police to charge and detain Indigenous people in circumstances "when a white person in the same circumstances might not be arrested at all, or might not be held." The inquiry explained that many police have come to view Indigenous people not as a community deserving protection but a community from which the rest of society must be protected. This has led to a situation often described as one of Indigenous people being "over-policed" but "under-protected."

Many Indigenous people feel they have little reason to trust police and as a consequence are reluctant to turn to police for protection. Police forces were used to enforce policies such as the removal of children to residential schools that have torn apart Indigenous communities. Today, many Indigenous people believe police are as likely to harm as to protect them. Amnesty International has previously drawn attention to incidents in which police in Canada have been responsible for, or are apparently implicated in, acts of violence against Indigenous people or apparent reckless disregard for their welfare and safety. These include the 1995 killing of land rights protestor Dudley George by an Ontario Provincial Police officer and the concern that police may have been involved in a series of freezing deaths of Indigenous men on the outskirts of Saskatoon.

The Saskatchewan Justice Reform Commission noted that "mothers of Aboriginal youth have spoken about the apprehension they feel when their children leave the home at night. Their fears involve the possibility of police abusing their children." One Indigenous woman, herself a professor at a Canadian university, told Amnesty International that she has instructed her teenage son to never talk to the police unless she is present.

Protesting against the absence of any permanent police force in many northern communities, the Inuit Women's Association of Canada has said, "In order to serve all parts of the communities, the police have to know our communities, they must be a part of our communities." Many police forces in Canada now require officers to take courses in cultural sensitivity, cross-cultural communication, or Indigenous history to help improve their understanding of Indigenous communities. Despite such requirements, the Saskatchewan Justice Reform Commission concluded, "Police officers continue to be assigned to First Nations and Métis communities with minimal knowledge of the culture and history of the people they serve."

Despite the efforts of many police forces to hire more Indigenous officers, Indigenous people are still underrepresented in police forces across Canada. Greater effort must be made to hire more Indigenous officers, especially women.

More attention must also be made to integrate an understanding of Indigenous communities into core learning experiences of all officers. For example, the concerns, perspectives, and needs of Indigenous communities should be reflected in the operational scenarios used in police training. Officers also need the time and the opportunity within their day-to-day duties to develop the necessary relationships of mutual understanding and trust with Indigenous communities. Unfortunately, many officers told Amnesty International that heavy workloads and frequent, often mandatory, rotations in and out of assignments, present real barriers to officers understanding and being trusted by Indigenous communities.

Police forces should work with Indigenous organizations to establish practices and policies that can support not only the learning of individual officers but also an improved relationship between Indigenous communities and the force as a whole. The Saskatchewan Justice Reform Commission pointed to a number of positive practices within the Saskatoon police force that it felt should be emulated elsewhere. These included the creation of an Indigenous liaison post and regular co-operation with community elders, including having elders accompany officers on some patrols in predominantly Indigenous neighbourhoods.

One of the critical areas for institutional reform highlighted by Amnesty International's research is the way police respond to reports of missing persons. Many Indigenous families told Amnesty International that police did little when they reported a sister or daughter missing and seemed to be waiting for the woman to be found. Police point out that the vast majority of people who are reported missing have run away or chosen to break off ties with family or friends. Most people who have voluntarily "gone missing" in this way do quickly turn up on their own.

However, this does not excuse incidents recounted to Amnesty International where, despite the concern of family members that a missing sister or daughter was in serious danger, police failed to take basic steps such as promptly interviewing family and friends or appealing to the public for information. These steps are particularly urgent when the missing person is a girl, as the state has special obligations to find and protect children at risk. However, every missing person report needs to be carefully assessed to determine the risk to the missing person. Unfortunately, even in large cities, many Canadian police forces do not have specialized personnel assigned to missing person cases. Instead, the task of assessing the risk and the credibility of the family's fears may fall to individual officers with little or no specific training or experience related to missing persons....

Because of the vital role they play in society, and the power they wield, it is critical that police be held accountable. That must include accountability for failing to fulfill their duties, as spelled out in official policies, to fully and impartially investigate all reports of threats to women's lives. That issue emerged as a clear concern in the course of research for this report. The families of missing and murdered women need to have greater formal access to the police, for example, through the appointment of community ombudspersons, to ensure that their concerns are addressed in an appropriate manner.

The Healing Journey:
Justice for Missing and Murdered Indigenous Women

All victims of violent crime have the right to justice. Under international human rights laws and standards, justice is not limited to the prosecution and punishment of the person who carried out the crime. Justice also includes a public acknowledgement of the crime, the opportunity and the ability for the victims of violence and their survivors to heal and to rebuild their lives, and assurance that the crime will not be repeated.

Although the formal court system cannot address all of these needs on its own, it nonetheless plays a vital role in assuring justice in the fullest sense of the word. The Saskatchewan Justice Reform Commission noted that the Canadian court system was imposed on Indigenous peoples without their consent and continues to be looked on with suspicion and mistrust by many. To establish trust in the court system, and ensure that court proceedings reflect an awareness and appreciation of the specific circumstances of Indigenous peoples, the commission recommended cross-cultural training for all judges and the appointment of Indigenous judges in every level of court....

It is important as well that Indigenous people who come in contact with the law, either as the accused or as victims, receive appropriate assistance in understanding the court system and having their voices heard. Amnesty International notes that in many jurisdictions across Canada a system of Indigenous court workers provides advocates to work on behalf of community members dealing with the justice system. Clear policies and protocols should also be established with respect to the timely provision of information, including autopsy results and coroners' reports, to the families of missing and murdered persons....

Official Indifference

While the federal and provincial governments in Canada can point to numerous programs undertaken to fulfill the rights of Indigenous peoples, the seriousness of these concerns requires that government do more.

Many of the families and frontline organizations interviewed for this report expressed concern and anger at the seeming indifference of Canadian officials and Canadian society for the welfare and safety of Indigenous women....

IV. NINE STOLEN SISTERS: CASE STUDIES OF DISCRIMINATION AND VIOLENCE AGAINST INDIGENOUS WOMEN IN CANADA

The following nine cases have been selected because they represent common themes that have emerged in the course of Amnesty International's research. They have been chosen because they reflect the variety of factors that appear to put Indigenous women at heightened risk. The root causes of discrimination and violence are often complex and are invariably interconnected. In some instances, it is quite clear that Indigenous women are either attacked by individuals or inadequately protected by authorities expressly because of their Indigenous identity. In some cases, the Indigenous women who have gone missing or been killed have been working in the sex trade and may have had addictions to alcohol or drugs.

All women in such circumstances, not only Indigenous women, face an increased risk of violence and discrimination. The risk that Indigenous women face in these circumstances is often exacerbated by racism and discrimination because of their Indigenous identity.

Amnesty International's research has also pointed to a variety of historical and current factors that have led a disproportionate number of Indigenous women into the sex trade, where they face that heightened risk. A number of the cases recounted in this report demonstrate, in human terms, the disturbing connections among past policies such as residential schools, societal discrimination against Indigenous people, involvement in the sex trade, and deadly violence.

These cases also represent two critical aspects of the reality of violence and discrimination against Indigenous women. In some instances, the violence itself is racist and sexist. In other cases, it may be the response from the police, other authorities, the media, and the general public that is racist and sexist. In yet other cases it is both.

Amnesty International is concerned that all of these dimensions to the problem of violence against Indigenous women give rise to serious human rights concerns, be it racist violence, discriminatory responses to violence, or the consequences of the many discriminatory laws, policies, and practices, past and present, that have led to the marginalization of Indigenous peoples in Canada. These cases all speak to the painful human cost of government failure to address those human rights concerns. All dimensions to the problem demand a response from governments across Canada. Yet the first case, a murder occurring more than thirty years ago that resulted in a provincial inquiry into the Manitoba justice system, is a stark reminder of the failure of governments to take adequate action to date.

An Unheeded Warning:
Helen Betty Osborne — Murdered November 12, 1971

There is one fundamental fact: her murder was a racist and sexist act. Betty Osborne would be alive today had she not been an Aboriginal woman.

Helen Betty Osborne was born in Norway House, a Cree community at the northern end of Lake Winnipeg in the Province of Manitoba. In 1969, at the age of seventeen, she left her community to pursue her education, with the dream of becoming a teacher and helping her people.

At the time, Indigenous children who wanted to graduate from high school had no choice but to leave their communities. The federal government, pursuing a policy of cultural assimilation — and having decided that Indigenous communities offered no future for young people — wanted Indigenous children to get their education in predominantly non-Indigenous towns and cities. In Norway House, the local school only provided the first eight of the twelve grades of public school.

For two years, Helen Betty Osborne attended the Guy Hill Residential School outside The Pas. Then, in 1971 she moved into The Pas to attend high school.

A provincial justice commission, which would later examine the circumstances surrounding the murder of Helen Betty Osborne, described The Pas, a town of about six thousand people in 1971, as being sharply divided between Indigenous and non-Indigenous residents. "At the movie theatre, each group sat on its own side; in at least one of the bars, Indians were not allowed to sit in certain areas; and in the school lunchroom, the two groups, Aboriginal and non-Aboriginal, ate apart."

According to the Manitoba Justice Inquiry, tensions between the two communities often turned violent, with police failing to inter-vene. There was also a pattern of sexual harassment of Indigenous women and girls. Police officers who testified before the inquiry described "white youths cruising the town, attempting to pick up Aboriginal girls for drinking parties and for sex." The inquiry found that the RCMP failed to check on the girls' safety. The Department of Indian Affairs also ignored the practice, failing to work with the schools to warn Indigenous students of the dangers.

On Friday, November 12, 1971, Helen Betty Osborne went out with a number of friends to a dance. At around 2:00 a.m., as she was walking back to house where she was billeted, she was accosted by four non-Indigenous men.

According to the testimony of one of the men, the four had decided to pick up an Indigenous woman for sex. When Osborne refused, they forced her into their car. In the car, she was beaten and sexually assaulted. She was then taken to a cabin owned by one of the men where she was beaten and stabbed to death. According to the autopsy report, she was severely beaten around the head and stabbed at least fifty times, possibly with a screwdriver.

Twenty years later, the Manitoba Justice Inquiry concluded that the murder of Helen Betty Osborne had been fuelled by racism and sexism:

> Women in our society live under a constant threat of violence. The death of Helen Betty Osborne was a brutal expression of that violence. She fell victim to vicious stereotypes born of ignorance and aggression when she was picked up by four drunken men looking for sex.

The inquiry also pointed out that the life of Helen Betty Osborne might have been saved if police had taken action on a pattern of threats to Indigenous women's safety that was already evident in 1971:

> We know that cruising for sex was a common prac-
> tice in The Pas in 1971. We know, too, that young
> Aboriginal women, often underage, were the usual
> objects of the practice. And we know that the
> RCMP did not feel that the practice necessitated
> any particular vigilance on its part.

According to the Justice Inquiry, racism also marred the initial RCMP investigation. Helen Betty Osborne's Indigenous friends were initially treated as suspects. Teenagers were interviewed without the consent or knowledge of their parents. One of Helen Betty Osborne's friends was taken out into the bush to be interrogated. When she hesitated in answering a question, police threw her over the hood of their car. They later took her to the morgue to see her friend's mutilated body. In contrast, police initially failed to act on a tip naming the four non-Indigenous men responsible who took part in the abduction. The men's car was not searched until at least a year later, and the Justice Inquiry noted that the car's owner was treated with extreme deference. Although police were eventually convinced that these four non-Indigenous men were responsible for the murder, unlike the Indigenous youths, they were not brought in for questioning.

By the end of 1972, the police concluded that they did not have enough evidence to go to trial. The case then lapsed for more than ten years until an officer placed an ad in the local paper asking for information on the case. This ad resulted in the discovery of new evidence on the basis of which the first charges were laid in October 1986. After these charges were laid, media coverage resulted in new information coming forward.

Finally, the first of the men charged agreed to testify in return for immunity from prosecution.

In December 1987, one of the four men, Dwayne Johnston, was sentenced to life imprisonment for the murder of Helen Betty Osborne. A second man was acquitted, while the other two men who were present during the abduction and murder were never charged.

The Justice Inquiry determined that the most important factor obstructing justice in this case was failure of members of the non-Indigenous community to bring forward evidence that would have assisted the investigation. The inquiry concluded that the community's silence was at least partly motivated by racism. The question remains, however, why the police waited more than ten years to publicly seek the assistance of the community.

Dwayne Johnston has been released from prison on parole. The family of Helen Betty Osborne has brought him into a traditional healing circle so that he can better understand the crime he committed. The family has since become convinced that Johnston, although responsible for a terrible crime, was not the principle instigator of the attack on Helen Betty Osborne.

The Manitoba Justice Inquiry put forward an extensive list of reforms to be undertaken to ensure that the justice system would provide Indigenous people the protection they needed and not contribute to further victimization. The recommendations were wide-ranging and required action from all levels of government. Recommendations included recognizing Indigenous peoples' right to self-government, establishing Indigenous legal systems, addressing outstanding land and resource disputes, recruiting more Indigenous police officers, ensuring independent procedures for investigation and resolution of complaints against police, establishing a special investigations unit to take control of the investigation of possible incidents of serious police misconduct, and increasing services to women escaping situations of violence. Amnesty International is of the view that adopting these recommendations in a manner consistent with international human rights standards would provide Indigenous women with greater protection from violence.

In a book published ten years after the inquiry made its final report, one of the former Commissioners complained that the federal government had not undertaken any of the recommended reforms within its jurisdiction while the provincial government was still at the stage of studying which recommendations to implement.

> The Aboriginal Justice Inquiry made over 150 recommendations. Almost none of them have been acted upon. There is either the inability to understand the need for improvements or the same century-long governmental inertia. The result is clear; Aboriginal people continue to suffer at the hands of an inappropriate justice system.

V. CONCLUSIONS AND RECOMMENDATIONS

No one should suffer the grief of having a sister, mother, or daughter suddenly disappear never to be seen again. No one should have to live in fear that they will be the next woman or girl to go missing.

Canadian officials have a clear and inescapable obligation to ensure the safety of Indigenous women, to bring those responsible for attacks against them to justice, and to address the deeper problems of marginalization, dispossession, and impoverishment that have placed so many Indigenous women in harm's way....

3

ROYAL COMMISSION ON ABORIGINAL PEOPLES (1996)

The 1983 publication of *Native Children and the Child Welfare System*, prepared for the Canadian Council on Social Development by Patrick Johnston, sent shock waves through child welfare and government systems, particularly those involved in First Nations child welfare. It presented documentary evidence that First Nations people had good grounds for protesting against the massive involvement of child welfare agencies in removing children from their families and communities.

Johnston adopted the phrase "Sixties Scoop" to describe a phenomenon that emerged in the years preceding his study. For example, he reported on the significant increase in the percentage of Aboriginal children in care in the Province of British Columbia:

> In 1955, there were 3,433 children in the care of
> British Columbia's child welfare branch. Of that

number, it was estimated that twenty-nine children, or less than 1 percent of the total, were of
Indian ancestry. By 1964, however, 1,446 children
in care in British Columbia were of Indian extrac-
tion. That number represented 34.2 percent of all
children in care. Within ten years, in other words,
the representation of Native children in British
Columbia's child welfare system had jumped
from almost nil to a third. It was a pattern being
repeated in other parts of Canada, as well.

The term *in care* refers to children in the care of child welfare
agencies for the purpose of protecting them from neglect or abuse.
Care may be provided in foster homes, adoption placements, or
in group or institutional settings. Johnston gathered data from
the federal department of Indian affairs and from provincial and
territorial ministries responsible for social services. Despite some
problems of comparability of data, his analysis showed consistent
overrepresentation of Aboriginal children in the child welfare system across the country, the percentage of children in the care of the
state being consistently higher than the percentage of Aboriginal
children in the total population. Comparisons were done using
two criteria:

- the proportion of Aboriginal children in care was
  compared to the proportion of Aboriginal children in
  the total child population; and
- the number of children in the care of the state, as a
  percentage of all Aboriginal children, was compared
  to the total number of children in care as a percentage
  of the total child population of Canada.

Within the general picture of overrepresentation there were wide regional variations. In 1981–82, the percentage of Aboriginal children in care, as a percentage of all children in care in various provinces, ranged from a low of 2.6 percent in Quebec to a high of 63 percent in Saskatchewan. Child-in-care rates in the Maritime Provinces were in the lower range: New Brunswick, 3.9 percent; Nova Scotia, 4.3 percent; and Prince Edward Island, 10.7 percent. An estimate of the number of Aboriginal children in care in Newfoundland and Labrador placed the rate at around 8 percent. Ontario's overall rate of 7.7 percent masked the fact that in Northern Ontario child welfare agencies the proportion of Aboriginal children in care was extremely high — an estimated 85 percent in the Kenora-Patricia agency, for example. Intermediate ranges were found in other western provinces: Manitoba, 32 percent; Alberta, 41 percent (including delinquent children on probation and children with disabilities receiving special services); and British Columbia, 36.7 percent. The Yukon, with 61 percent, still had overrepresentation of Aboriginal children despite the higher proportion of Aboriginal children in the general population. The Northwest Territories, with First Nations, Métis, and Inuit children making up 45 percent of children in care, was the only jurisdiction where the representation of Aboriginal children was not disproportionate.

When the number of Aboriginal children in care is considered as a proportion of all Aboriginal children, the percentage of children in care ranged from a low of 1.8 percent in the Northwest Territories to a high of 5.9 percent in British Columbia. Across Canada, on average, 4.6 percent of Aboriginal children were in agency care in 1980–81, compared to just under 1 percent of the general Canadian child population.

Information on where children in care were placed, whether in Aboriginal homes or non-Aboriginal foster and adoption homes, was not available for all provinces. In most provinces, however, placements in non-Aboriginal homes typically ranged from 70 percent to 90 percent, with the exception of Quebec, where Cree and Inuit child placements, reported separately, were almost entirely in Aboriginal homes, usually in the children's home communities. Approximately half the other Aboriginal children in care in Quebec were placed in non-Aboriginal homes.

Increased activity on the part of child welfare agencies corresponded with the federal government's decision to expand its role in funding social welfare services and phase out residential schools, which in the 1960s had increasingly assumed the role of caring for children in "social need."

It was already accepted at the time in the professional community that apprehension should be strictly a last resort in protecting children from harm and that Aboriginal children were particularly vulnerable to its harmful effects. Johnston explains:

> Many experts in the child welfare field are coming to believe that the removal of any child from his/her parents is inherently damaging, in and of itself.... The effects of apprehension on an individual Native child will often be much more traumatic than for his non-Native counterpart. Frequently, when the Native child is taken from his parents, he is also removed from a tightly knit community of extended family members and neighbours, who may have provided some support. In addition, he is removed from a unique, distinctive and familiar culture. The Native child is placed in a position of triple jeopardy.

Later analysts echoed Johnston's criticism that the interventions of social agencies reflected colonial attitudes and attempts to assimilate Aboriginal children and continue the work begun by residential schools. Hudson and McKenzie argued that the child welfare system devalued Aboriginal culture by not recognizing and using traditional Aboriginal systems of child protection, making judgments about child care based on dominant Canadian norms, and persistently using non-Aboriginal foster and adoption placements.

In a research report prepared for this commission, Joyce Timpson, a social worker with extensive experience in northwestern Ontario, suggests that the colonialist and assimilationist explanation of the Sixties Scoop may underplay the reality that Aboriginal families were dealing with the severe disruption caused by social, economic, and cultural changes. In many communities, they were also coping with the stress of relocation. Timpson presents strong evidence suggesting that the federal government's willingness to pay child-in-care costs, along with federal and provincial governments' resistance to supporting preventive services, family counselling, or rehabilitation, were major factors in making apprehension and permanent removal of children the treatment applied most often in problem situations....

Another milestone in the history of Aboriginal child welfare was the 1985 report of an inquiry by Justice Edwin C. Kimelman on adoptions and placements of First Nations and Métis children from Manitoba. The inquiry was prompted by protests from the Aboriginal community against placement of First Nations and Métis children in adoptive homes in the United States. Justice Kimelman found that the highly publicized case of Cameron Kerley was only one instance of a system gone awry....

Justice Kimelman's report validated for the people of Manitoba and Canadians at large the pain and suffering being inflicted on First Nations and Métis families and children. To First Nations people, his report constituted an indictment of child welfare services:

The failures of the child welfare system have been made known many years after the fact in the statistics from correctional institutions, psychiatric hospitals, and as former wards of agencies became neglectful and abusive, parents themselves....

In 1982, no one, except the Indian and the Métis people really believed the reality — that Native children were routinely being shipped to adoption homes in the United States and to other provinces in Canada. Every social worker, every administrator, and every agency or region viewed the situation from a narrow perspective and saw each individual case as an exception, as a case involving extenuating circumstances. No one fully comprehended that 25 percent of all children placed for adoption were placed outside of Manitoba. No one fully comprehended that virtually all those children were of Native descent....

Children who entered the [child welfare] system were generally lost to family and community — or were returned with there having been little input to change the situation from which they were taken in the first place....

Every facet of the system examined by the commission revealed evidence of a program rooted in antiquity and resistant to change.

An abysmal lack of sensitivity to children and families was revealed. Families approached agencies for help and found that what was described as being in the child's "best interest" resulted in their families being torn asunder and siblings separated. Social workers grappled with cultural patterns far different than their own with no preparation and no opportunities to gain understanding. It was expected that workers would get their training in the field.

The agencies complained of a lack of adequate resources, and central directorate staff complained of a lack of imaginative planning for children by agencies....

The funding mechanisms perpetuated existing service patterns and stifled, even prevented, innovative approaches. There was little statistical data and, what there was, was next to useless for program planning purposes. There was no follow-up on adoptions and thus no way to gather the data upon which any kind of evaluation of the adoption program could be based....

The appalling reality is that everyone involved believed they were doing their best and stood firm in their belief that the system was working well.... The miracle is that there were not more children lost in this system run by so many well-intentioned people. The road to hell was paved with good intentions and the child welfare system was the paving contractor.

4

TRUTH AND RECONCILIATION COMMISSION FINAL REPORT (2015)

INTRODUCTION

For over a century, the central goals of Canada's Aboriginal policy were to eliminate Aboriginal governments; ignore Aboriginal rights; terminate the Treaties; and, through a process of assimilation, cause Aboriginal peoples to cease to exist as distinct legal, social, cultural, religious, and racial entities in Canada. The establishment and operation of residential schools were a central element of this policy, which can best be described as "cultural genocide."

Physical genocide is the mass killing of the members of a targeted group, and *biological genocide* is the destruction of the group's reproductive capacity. *Cultural genocide* is the destruction of those structures and practices that allow the group to continue as a group. States that engage in cultural genocide set out to destroy the political and social institutions of the targeted group. Land is seized, and populations are forcibly transferred and their movement is restricted. Languages are banned. Spiritual leaders are persecuted, spiritual practices are forbidden, and objects of spiritual value are confiscated and destroyed. And, most significantly to the issue at hand, families are disrupted to prevent the transmission of cultural values and identity from one generation to the next.

In its dealing with Aboriginal people, Canada did all these things.

Canada asserted control over Aboriginal land. In some locations, Canada negotiated Treaties with First Nations; in others, the land was simply occupied or seized. The negotiation of Treaties, while seemingly honourable and legal, was often marked by fraud and coercion, and Canada was, and remains, slow to implement their provisions and intent.

On occasion, Canada forced First Nations to relocate their reserves from agriculturally valuable or resource-rich land onto remote and economically marginal reserves.

Without legal authority or foundation, in the 1880s Canada instituted a "pass system" that was intended to confine First Nations people to their reserves.

Canada replaced existing forms of Aboriginal government with relatively powerless band councils whose decisions it could override and whose leaders it could depose. In the process, it disempowered Aboriginal women, who had held significant influence and powerful roles in many First Nations, including the Mohawks, the Carrier, and Tlingit.

Canada denied the right to participate fully in Canadian political, economic, and social life to those Aboriginal people who refused to abandon their Aboriginal identity.

Canada outlawed Aboriginal spiritual practices, jailed Aboriginal spiritual leaders, and confiscated sacred objects.

And, Canada separated children from their parents, sending them to residential schools. This was done not to educate them but primarily to break their link to their culture and identity. In justifying the government's residential school policy, Canada's first prime minister, Sir John A. Macdonald, told the House of Commons in 1883:

> When the school is on the reserve, the child lives with its parents, who are savages; he is surrounded by savages, and though he may learn to read and write, his habits and training and mode of thought are Indian. He is simply a savage who can read and write. It has been strongly pressed on myself, as the head of the Department, that Indian children should be withdrawn as much as possible from the parental influence, and the only way to do that would be to put them in central training industrial schools where they will acquire the habits and modes of thought of white men.

These measures were part of a coherent policy to eliminate Aboriginal people as distinct peoples and to assimilate them into the Canadian mainstream against their will. Deputy Minister of Indian Affairs Duncan Campbell Scott outlined the goals of that policy in 1920, when he told a parliamentary committee that "our object is to continue until there is not a single Indian in Canada that has not been absorbed into the body politic." These goals were reiterated in 1969 in the federal government's Statement on Indian Policy (more often referred to as the "White Paper"), which sought to end Indian status and terminate the Treaties that the federal government had negotiated with First Nations.

The Canadian government pursued this policy of cultural genocide because it wished to divest itself of its legal and financial obligations to Aboriginal people and gain control over their land and resources. If every Aboriginal person had been "absorbed into the body politic," there would be no reserves, no Treaties, and no Aboriginal rights.

Residential schooling quickly became a central element in the federal government's Aboriginal policy. When Canada was created as a country in 1867, Canadian churches were already operating a small number of boarding schools for Aboriginal people. As settlement moved westward in the 1870s, Roman Catholic and Protestant missionaries established missions and small boarding schools across the Prairies, in the North, and in British Columbia. Most of these schools received small, per-student grants from the federal government. In 1883, the federal government moved to establish three, large, residential schools for First Nation children in western Canada. In the following years, the system grew dramatically. According to the Indian Affairs annual report for 1930, there were eighty residential schools in operation across the country. The Indian Residential Schools Settlement Agreement provided compensation to students who attended 139 residential schools and residences. The federal government has estimated that at least 150,000 First Nation, Métis, and Inuit students passed through the system.

Roman Catholic, Anglican, United, Methodist, and Presbyterian churches were the major denominations involved in the administration of the residential school system. The government's partnership with the churches remained in place until 1969, and, although most of the schools had closed by the 1980s, the last federally supported residential schools remained in operation until the late 1990s.

For children, life in these schools was lonely and alien. Buildings were poorly located, poorly built, and poorly maintained. The staff was limited in numbers, often poorly trained, and not adequately supervised. Many schools were poorly heated and poorly ventilated, and the diet was meagre and of poor quality. Discipline was harsh, and daily life was highly regimented. Aboriginal languages and cultures were denigrated and suppressed.

The educational goals of the schools were limited and confused, and usually reflected a low regard for the intellectual capabilities of Aboriginals. For the students, education and technical training too often gave way to the drudgery of doing the chores necessary to make the schools self-sustaining. Child neglect was institutionalized, and the lack of supervision created situations where students were prey to sexual and physical abusers.

In establishing residential schools, the Canadian government essentially declared Aboriginal people to be unfit parents. Aboriginal parents were labelled as being indifferent to the future of their children — a judgment contradicted by the fact that parents often kept their children out of schools because they saw those schools, quite accurately, as dangerous and harsh institutions that sought to raise their children in alien ways. Once in the schools, brothers and sisters were kept apart, and the government and churches even arranged marriages for students after they finished their education.

The residential school system was based on an assumption that European civilization and Christian religions were superior to Aboriginal culture, which was seen as being savage and brutal. Government officials also were insistent that children be discouraged — and often prohibited — from speaking their own languages. The missionaries who ran the schools played prominent roles in the church-led campaigns to ban Aboriginal spiritual practices such as the Potlatch and the Sun Dance (more properly called the "Thirst Dance"), and to end traditional Aboriginal marriage practices. Although, in most of their official pronouncements, government and church officials took the position that Aboriginal people could be civilized, it is clear that many believed that Aboriginal culture was inherently inferior.

This hostility to Aboriginal cultural and spiritual practice continued well into the twentieth century. In 1942, John House, the principal of the Anglican school in Gleichen, Alberta, became involved in a campaign to have two Blackfoot chiefs deposed, in part because of their support for traditional dance ceremonies. In 1947, Roman Catholic official J.O. Plourde told a federal parliamentary committee that since Canada was a Christian nation that was committed to having "all its citizens belonging to one or other of the Christian churches," he could see no reason why the residential schools "should foster Aboriginal beliefs." United Church official George Dorey told the same committee that he questioned whether there was such a thing as "Native religion."

Into the 1950s and 1960s, the prime mission of residential schools was the cultural transformation of Aboriginal children. In 1953, J.E. Andrews, the principal of the Presbyterian school in Kenora, Ontario, wrote that "we must face realistically the fact that the only hope for the Canadian Indian is eventual assimilation into the white race." The goal of residential schooling was to separate children from their families, culture, and identity. In 1957, the principal of the Gordon's Reserve school in Saskatchewan, Albert Southard, wrote that he believed that the goal of residential schooling was to "change the philosophy of the Indian child. In other words since they must work and live with 'whites' then they must begin to think as 'whites.'" Southard said that the Gordon's school could never have a student council, since "in so far as the Indian understands the department's policy, he is against it." In a 1958 article on residential schools, senior Oblate Andre Renaud echoed the words of John A. Macdonald, arguing that when students at day schools went back to their "homes at the end of the school day and for the weekend, the pupils are re-exposed to their Native culture, however diluted, from which the school is trying to separate them." A residential school, on the other hand, could "surround its pupils almost twenty-four hours a day with non-Indian Canadian culture through radio, television, public address system, movies, books, newspapers, group activities, etc."

Despite the coercive measures that the government adopted, it failed to achieve its policy goals. Although Aboriginal peoples and cultures have been badly damaged, they continue to exist. Aboriginal people have refused to surrender their identity. It was the former students, the Survivors of Canada's residential schools, who placed the residential school issue on the public agenda. Their efforts led to the negotiation of the Indian Residential Schools Settlement Agreement that mandated the establishment of a residential school Truth and Reconciliation Commission of Canada (TRC).

The Survivors acted with courage and determination. We should do no less. It is time to commit to a process of reconciliation. By establishing a new and respectful relationship, we restore what must be restored, repair what must be repaired, and return what must be returned.

RECONCILIATION AT THE CROSSROADS

To some people, reconciliation is the re-establishment of a conciliatory state. However, this is a state that many Aboriginal people assert never has existed between Aboriginal and non-Aboriginal people. To others, reconciliation, in the context of Indian residential schools, is similar to dealing with a situation of family violence. It's about coming to terms with events of the past in a manner that overcomes conflict and establishes a respectful and healthy relationship among people, going forward. It is in the latter context that the Truth and Reconciliation Commission of Canada has approached the question of reconciliation.

To the Commission, reconciliation is about establishing and maintaining a mutually respectful relationship between Aboriginal and non-Aboriginal peoples in this country. In order for that to happen, there has to be awareness of the past harm that has been inflicted, atonement for the causes, and action to change behaviour.

We are not there yet. The relationship between Aboriginal and non-Aboriginal peoples is not a mutually respectful one. But, we believe we can get there, and we believe we can maintain it. Our ambition is to show how we can do that.

In 1996, the Report of the Royal Commission on Aboriginal Peoples urged Canadians to begin a national process of reconciliation that would have set the country on a bold new path, fundamentally changing the very foundations of Canada's relationship with Aboriginal peoples. Much of what the Royal Commission had to say has been ignored by government; a majority of its recommendations were never implemented. But the report and its findings opened people's eyes and changed the conversation about the reality for Aboriginal people in this country.

In 2015, as the Truth and Reconciliation Commission of Canada wraps up its work, the country has a rare second chance to seize a lost opportunity for reconciliation. We live in a twenty-first-century global world. At stake is Canada's place as a prosperous, just, and inclusive democracy within that global world. At the TRC's first National Event in Winnipeg, Manitoba, in 2010, residential school Survivor Alma Mann Scott said,

> The healing is happening — the reconciliation....
> I feel that there's some hope for us not just as Canadians but for the world, because I know I'm not the only one. I know that Anishinaabe people across Canada, First Nations, are not the only ones. My brothers and sisters in New Zealand, Australia, Ireland — there's different areas of the world where this type of stuff happened.... I don't

> see it happening in a year, but we can start making
> changes to laws and to education systems ... so
> that we can move forward.

Reconciliation must support Aboriginal peoples as they heal from the destructive legacies of colonization that have wreaked such havoc in their lives. But it must do even more. Reconciliation must inspire Aboriginal and non-Aboriginal peoples to transform Canadian society so that our children and grandchildren can live together in dignity, peace, and prosperity on these lands we now share.

The urgent need for reconciliation runs deep in Canada. Expanding public dialogue and action on reconciliation beyond residential schools will be critical in the coming years. Although some progress has been made, significant barriers to reconciliation remain. The relationship between the federal government and Aboriginal peoples is deteriorating. Instead of moving toward reconciliation, there have been divisive conflicts over Aboriginal education, child welfare, and justice. The daily news has been filled with reports of controversial issues ranging from the call for a national inquiry on violence toward Aboriginal women and girls to the impact of the economic development of lands and resources on Treaties and Aboriginal title and rights. The courts continue to hear Aboriginal rights cases, and new litigation has been filed by Survivors of day schools not covered under the Indian Residential Schools Settlement Agreement, as well as by victims of the "Sixties Scoop," which was a child-welfare policy that removed Aboriginal children from their homes and placed them with non-Aboriginal families. The promise of reconciliation, which seemed so imminent back in 2008 when the prime minister, on behalf of all Canadians, apologized to Survivors, has faded. Too many Canadians know little or nothing about the deep historical roots of these conflicts. This lack of historical knowledge has serious consequences for

First Nations, Inuit, and Métis peoples, and for Canada as a whole. In government circles, it makes for poor public policy decisions. In the public realm, it reinforces racist attitudes and fuels civic distrust between Aboriginal peoples and other Canadians.

Too many Canadians still do not know the history of Aboriginal peoples' contributions to Canada, or understand that by virtue of the historical and modern Treaties negotiated by our government, we are all Treaty people. History plays an important role in reconciliation; to build for the future, Canadians must look to, and learn from, the past.

As Commissioners, we understood from the start that although reconciliation could not be achieved during the TRC's lifetime, the country could and must take ongoing positive and concrete steps forward. While the Commission has been a catalyst for deepening our national awareness of the meaning and potential of reconciliation, it will take many heads, hands, and hearts, working together, at all levels of society to maintain momentum in the years ahead. It will also take sustained political will at all levels of government and concerted material resources.

The thousands of Survivors who publicly shared their residential school experiences at TRC events in every region of this country have launched a much-needed dialogue about what is necessary to heal themselves, their families, communities, and the nation. Canadians have much to benefit from listening to the voices, experiences, and wisdom of Survivors, Elders, and Traditional Knowledge Keepers — and much more to learn about reconciliation. Aboriginal peoples have an important contribution to make to reconciliation. Their knowledge systems, oral histories, laws, and connections to the land have vitally informed the reconciliation process to date, and are essential to its ongoing progress.

At a Traditional Knowledge Keepers Forum sponsored by the TRC, Anishinaabe Elder Mary Deleary spoke about the responsibility for reconciliation that both Aboriginal and non-Aboriginal people carry. She emphasized that the work of reconciliation must continue in ways that honour the ancestors, respect the land, and rebalance relationships. She said,

> I'm so filled with belief and hope because when I hear your voices at the table, I hear and know that the responsibilities that our ancestors carried ... are still being carried ... even through all of the struggles, even through all of what has been disrupted ... we can still hear the voice of the land. We can hear the care and love for the children. We can hear about our law. We can hear about our stories, our governance, our feasts, [and] our medicines.... We have work to do. That work we are [already] doing as [Aboriginal] peoples. Our relatives who have come from across the water [non-Aboriginal people], you still have work to do on your road.... The land is made up of the dust of our ancestors' bones. And so to reconcile with this land and everything that has happened, there is much work to be done ... in order to create balance.

At the Victoria Regional Event in 2012, Survivor Archie Little said,

> [For] me reconciliation is righting a wrong. And how do we do that? All these people in this room, a lot of non-Aboriginals, a lot of Aboriginals that probably didn't go to residential school; we need to work together.... My mother had a high standing in our cultural ways. We lost that. It

> was taken away.... And I think it's time for you
> non-Aboriginals ... to go to your politicians and
> tell them that we have to take responsibility for
> what happened. We have to work together.

The Reverend Stan McKay of the United Church, who is
also a Survivor, believes that reconciliation can happen only when
everyone accepts responsibility for healing in ways that foster
respect. He said,

> [There must be] a change in perspective about
> the way in which Aboriginal peoples would be
> engaged with Canadian society in the quest for
> reconciliation.... [We cannot] perpetuate the
> paternalistic concept that only Aboriginal peoples
> are in need of healing.... The perpetrators are
> wounded and marked by history in ways that
> are different from the victims, but both groups
> require healing.... How can a conversation about
> reconciliation take place if all involved do not
> adopt an attitude of humility and respect? ... We
> all have stories to tell and in order to grow in tol-
> erance and understanding we must listen to the
> stories of others.

Over the past five years, the Truth and Reconciliation
Commission of Canada urged Canadians not to wait until our
final report was issued before contributing to the reconciliation
process. We have been encouraged to see that across the country,
many people have been answering that call.

The youth of this country are taking up the challenge of reconciliation. Aboriginal and non-Aboriginal youth who attended TRC

National Events made powerful statements about why reconciliation matters to them. At the Alberta National Event in Edmonton in March 2014, an Indigenous youth spoke on behalf of a national Indigenous and non-Indigenous collaboration known as the "4Rs Youth Movement." Jessica Bolduc said,

> We have re-examined our thoughts and beliefs around colonialism, and have made a commitment to unpack our own baggage, and to enter into a new relationship with each other, using this momentum, to move our country forward, in light of the 150th anniversary of the Confederation of Canada in 2017.
>
> At this point in time, we ask ourselves, "What does that anniversary mean for us, as Indigenous youth and non-Indigenous youth, and how do we arrive at that day with something we can celebrate together?" … Our hope is that, one day, we will live together, as recognized nations, within a country we can all be proud of.

In 2013, at the British Columbia National Event in Vancouver, where over five thousand elementary and secondary school students attended Education Day, several non-Aboriginal youth talked about what they had learned. Matthew Meneses said, "I'll never forget this day. This is the first day they ever told us about residential schools. If I were to see someone who's Aboriginal, I'd ask them if they can speak their language because I think speaking their language is a pretty cool thing." Antonio Jordao said, "It makes me sad for those kids. They took them away from their homes — it was torture, it's not fair. They took them away from their homes. I don't agree with that. It's really wrong. That's one of the worst things that Canada did." Cassidy Morris said, "It's good that we're finally learning about what happened." Jacqulyn Byers told us, "I hope that events like this are able to bring closure to the horrible things that happened, and that a whole lot of people now recognize that the crime happened and that we need to make amends for it."

At the same National Event, TRC Honorary Witness Patsy George paid tribute to the strength of Aboriginal women and their contributions to the reconciliation process despite the oppression and violence they have experienced. She said,

> Women have always been a beacon of hope for me. Mothers and grandmothers in the lives of our children, and in the survival of our communities, must be recognized and supported. The justified rage we all feel and share today must be turned into instruments of transformation of our hearts and our souls, clearing the ground for respect, love, honesty, humility, wisdom, and truth. We owe it to all those who suffered, and we owe it to the children of today and tomorrow. May this day and the days ahead bring us peace and justice.

Aboriginal and non-Aboriginal Canadians from all walks of life spoke to us about the importance of reaching out to one another in ways that create hope for a better future. Whether one is First Nations, Inuit, Métis, a descendant of European settlers, a member of a minority group that suffered historical discrimination in Canada, or a new Canadian, we all inherit both the benefits and obligations of Canada. We are all Treaty people who share responsibility for taking action on reconciliation.

Without truth, justice, and healing, there can be no genuine reconciliation. Reconciliation is not about "closing a sad chapter of Canada's past," but about opening new healing pathways of reconciliation that are forged in truth and justice. We are mindful that knowing the truth about what happened in residential schools in and of itself does not necessarily lead to reconciliation. Yet, the importance of truth telling in its own right should not be underestimated; it restores the human dignity of victims of violence and calls governments and citizens to account. Without truth, justice is not served, healing cannot happen, and there can be no genuine reconciliation between Aboriginal and non-Aboriginal peoples in Canada. Speaking to us at the Traditional Knowledge Keepers Forum in June of 2014, Elder Dave Courchene posed a critical question: "When you talk about truth, whose truth are you talking about?"

The Commission's answer to Elder Courchene's question is that by truth, we mean not only the truth revealed in government and church residential school documents but also the truth of lived experiences as told to us by Survivors and others in their statements to this Commission. Together, these public testimonies constitute a new oral history record, one based on Indigenous legal traditions and the practice of witnessing. As people gathered at various TRC National Events and Community Hearings, they shared the experiences of truth telling and of offering expressions of reconciliation.

Over the course of its work, the Commission inducted a growing circle of TRC Honorary Witnesses. Their role has been to bear official witness to the testimonies of Survivors and their families, former school staff and their descendants, government and church officials, and any others whose lives have been affected by the residential schools. Beyond the work of the TRC, the Honorary Witnesses have pledged their commitment to the ongoing work of reconciliation between Aboriginal and non-Aboriginal peoples. We also encouraged everyone who attended TRC National Events or Community Hearings to see themselves as witnesses also, with an obligation to find ways of making reconciliation a concrete reality in their own lives, communities, schools, and workplaces.

As Elder Jim Dumont explained at the Traditional Knowledge Keepers Forum in June 2014, "in Ojibwe thinking, to speak the truth is to actually speak from the heart." At the Community Hearing in Key First Nation, Saskatchewan, in 2012, Survivor Wilfred Whitehawk told us he was glad that he disclosed his abuse.

> I don't regret it because it taught me something.
> It taught me to talk about truth, about me, to
> be honest about who I am.... I am very proud
> of who I am today. It took me a long time, but
> I'm there. And what I have, my values and belief
> systems are mine and no one is going to impose
> theirs on me. And no one today is going to take
> advantage of me, man or woman, the govern-
> ment or the RCMP, because I have a voice today.
> I can speak for me and no one can take that away.

Survivor and the child of Survivors Vitaline Elsie Jenner said, "I'm quite happy to be able to share my story.... I want the people of Canada to hear, to listen, for it is the truth.... I also want my grandchildren to learn, to learn from me that, yes, it did happen."

Another descendant of Survivors, Daniel Elliot, told the Commission,

> I think all Canadians need to stop and take a
> look and not look away. Yeah, it's embarrassing,
> yeah, it's an ugly part of our history. We don't
> want to know about it. What I want to see from
> the Commission is to rewrite the history books so
> that other generations will understand and not go

through the same thing that we're going through
now, like it never happened.

President of the Métis National Council Clement Chartier
spoke to the Commission about the importance of truth to justice
and reconciliation. At the Saskatchewan National Event, he said,

> The truth is important. So I'll try to address the
> truth and a bit of reconciliation as well. The truth
> is that the Métis Nation, represented by the Métis
> National Council, is not a party to the Indian
> Residential Schools Settlement Agreement.... And
> the truth is that the exclusion of the Métis Nation
> or the Métis as a people is reflected throughout this
> whole period not only in the Indian Residential
> Schools Settlement Agreement but in the apology
> made by Canada as well....
>
> We are, however, the products ... of the same
> assimilationist policy that the federal government
> foisted upon the Treaty Indian kids. So there
> ought to be some solution.... The Métis board-
> ing schools, residential schools, are excluded. And
> we need to ensure that everyone was aware of that
> and hopefully some point down the road, you will
> help advocate and get, you know, the governments
> or whoever is responsible to accept responsibility
> and to move forward on a path to reconciliation,
> because reconciliation should be for all Aboriginal
> peoples and not only some Aboriginal peoples.

At the British Columbia National Event, the former lieutenant
governor of British Columbia, the Honourable Steven Point, said,

And so many of you have said today, so many of
the witnesses that came forward said, "I cannot
forgive. I'm not ready to forgive." And I wondered
why. Reconciliation is about hearing the truth,
that's for sure. It's also about acknowledging that
truth. Acknowledging that what you've said is true.
Accepting responsibility for your pain and putting
those children back in the place they would have
been, had they not been taken from their homes....

What are the blockages to reconciliation? The
continuing poverty in our communities and the
failure of our government to recognize that "Yes, we
own the land." Stop the destruction of our territories and for God's sake, stop the deaths of so many
of our women on highways across this country....
I'm going to continue to talk about reconciliation,
but just as important, I'm going to foster healing in
our own people, so that our children can avoid this
pain, can avoid this destruction and finally, take
our rightful place in this "Our Canada."

When former residential school staff attended public TRC
events, some thought it was most important to hear directly from
Survivors, even if their own perspectives and memories of the
schools might differ from those of the Survivors. At a Community
Hearing in Thunder Bay, Ontario, Merle Nisley, who worked at
the Poplar Hill residential school in the early 1970s, said,

I think it would be valuable for people who have
been involved in the schools to hear stories per-
sonally. And I also think it would be valuable,
when it's appropriate ... [for] former students

who are on the healing path to ... hear some
of our stories, or to hear some of our perspectives. But I know that's a very difficult thing to
do.... Certainly this is not the time to try to ask
all those former students to sit and listen to the
rationale of the former staff because there's just
too much emotion there ... and there's too little
trust ... you can't do things like that when there's
low levels of trust. So I think really a very important thing is for former staff to hear the stories and
to be courageous enough just to hear them....
Where wrongs were done, where abuses happened, where punishment was over the top, and
wherever sexual abuse happened, somehow we
need to courageously sit and talk about that, and
apologize. I don't know how that will happen.

Nisley's reflections highlight one of the difficulties the
Commission faced in trying to create a space for respectful dialogue
between former residential school students and staff. While, in most
cases, this was possible, in other instances, Survivors and their family
members found it very difficult to listen to former staff, particularly
if they perceived the speaker to be an apologist for the schools.

At the TRC Victoria Regional Event, Brother Tom Cavanaugh,
the district superior of the Oblates of Mary Immaculate for British
Columbia and the Yukon, spoke about his time as a supervisor at
the Christie residential school.

What I experienced over the six years I was at
Christie residential school was a staff, Native and
non-Native alike, working together to provide as
much as possible, a safe loving environment for

the children attending Christie school. Was it a
perfect situation? No, it wasn't a perfect situation
… but again, there didn't seem to be, at that time,
any other viable alternative in providing a good
education for so many children who lived in relatively small and isolated communities.

Survivors and family members who were present in the audience spoke out, saying, "Truth, tell the truth." Brother Cavanaugh
replied, "If you give me a chance, I will tell you the truth." When
TRC Chair Justice Murray Sinclair intervened to ask the audience
to allow Brother Cavanaugh to finish his statement, he was able
to do so without further interruption. Visibly shaken, Cavanaugh
then went on to acknowledge that children had also been abused
in the schools, and he condemned such actions, expressing his sorrow and regret for this breach of trust.

I can honestly say that our men are hurting, too,
because of the abuse scandal and the rift that this
has created between First Nations and church
representatives. Many of our men who are still
working with First Nations have attended various truth and reconciliation sessions as well as
Returning to Spirit sessions, hoping to bring
about healing for all concerned. The Oblates
desire healing for the abused and for all touched
by the past breach of trust. It is our hope that
together we can continue to build a better society.

Later that same day, Ina Seitcher, who attended the Christie
residential school, painted a very different picture of the school
from what Brother Cavanaugh had described.

I went to Christie residential school. This morning
I heard a priest talking about his Christie residential school. I want to tell him [about] my Christie
residential school. I went there for ten months. Ten
months that impacted my life for fifty years. I am just
now on my healing journey.... I need to do this, I
need to speak out. I need to speak for my mom and
dad who went to residential school, for my aunts,
my uncles, all that are beyond now.... All the pain
of our people, the hurt, the anger.... That priest
that talked about how loving that Christie residential school was — it was not. That priest was most
likely in his office not knowing what was going on
down in the dorms or in the lunchroom.... There
were things that happened at Christie residential
school, and like I said, I'm just starting my healing
journey. There are doors that I don't even want to
open. I don't even want to open those doors because
I don't know what it would do to me.

These two, seemingly irreconcilable, truths are a stark reminder
that there are no easy shortcuts to reconciliation. The fact that there
were few direct exchanges at TRC events between Survivors and
former school staff indicates that for many, the time for reconciliation had not yet arrived. Indeed, for some, it may never arrive. At
the Manitoba National Event in 2010, Survivor Evelyn Brockwood
talked about why it is important to ensure that there is adequate time
for healing to occur in the truth and reconciliation process. She said,

When this came out at the beginning, I believe it
was 1990, about residential schools, people coming out with their stories, and ... I thought the

> term, the words they were using, were truth, heal-
> ing, and reconciliation. But somehow it seems
> like we are going from truth telling to reconcili-
> ation, to reconcile with our white brothers and
> sisters. My brothers and sisters, we have a lot of
> work to do in the middle. We should really lift
> up the word healing.... Go slow, we are going
> too fast, too fast.... We have many tears to shed
> before we even get to the word reconciliation.

To determine the truth and to tell the full and complete story of residential schools in this country, the TRC needed to hear from Survivors and their families, former staff, government and church officials, and all those affected by residential schools. Canada's national history in the future must be based on the truth about what happened in the residential schools. One hundred years from now, our children's children and their children must know and still remember this history, because they will inherit from us the responsibility of ensuring that it never happens again.

WHAT IS RECONCILIATION?

During the course of the Commission's work, it has become clear that the concept of reconciliation means different things to differ-ent people, communities, institutions, and organizations. The TRC mandate describes reconciliation as "an ongoing individual and col-lective process, and will require commitment from all those affected including First Nations, Inuit, and Métis former Indian Residential School (IRS) students, their families, communities, religious entities, former school employees, government, and the people of Canada. Reconciliation may occur between any of the above groups."

The Commission defines *reconciliation* as an ongoing process of establishing and maintaining respectful relationships. A critical part of this process involves repairing damaged trust by making apologies, providing individual and collective reparations, and following through with concrete actions that demonstrate real societal change. Establishing respectful relationships also requires the revitalization of Indigenous law and legal traditions. It is important that all Canadians understand how traditional First Nations, Inuit, and Métis approaches to resolving conflict, repairing harm, and restoring relationships can inform the reconciliation process.

Traditional Knowledge Keepers and Elders have long dealt with conflicts and harms using spiritual ceremonies and peacemaking practices, and by retelling oral history stories that reveal how their ancestors restored harmony to families and communities. These traditions and practices are the foundation of Indigenous law; they contain wisdom and practical guidance for moving toward reconciliation across this land.

As First Nations, Inuit, and Métis communities access and revitalize their spirituality, cultures, languages, laws, and governance systems, and as non-Aboriginal Canadians increasingly come to understand Indigenous history within Canada, and to recognize and respect Indigenous approaches to establishing and maintaining respectful relationships, Canadians can work together to forge a new covenant of reconciliation.

Despite the ravages of colonialism, every Indigenous nation across the country, each with its own distinctive culture and language, has kept its legal traditions and peacemaking practices alive in its communities. While Elders and Knowledge Keepers across the land have told us that there is no specific word for "reconciliation" in their own languages, there are many words, stories, and songs, as well as sacred objects such as wampum belts, peace pipes, eagle down, cedar boughs, drums, and regalia, that are used to establish relationships, repair conflicts, restore harmony, and make peace. The ceremonies and protocols of Indigenous law are still remembered and practised in many Aboriginal communities.

At the TRC Traditional Knowledge Keepers Forum in June 2014, TRC Survivor Committee member and Elder Barney Williams told us that from sea to sea,

> We hear words that allude to ... what is recon-
> ciliation? What does healing or forgiveness mean?
> And how there's parallels to all those words that
> the Creator gave to all the nations.... When I lis-
> ten and reflect on the voices of the ancestors, your
> ancestors, I hear my ancestor alluding to the same
> thing with a different dialect.... My understand-
> ing [of reconciliation] comes from a place and
> time when there was no English spoken ... from
> my grandmother who was born in the 1800s....
> I really feel privileged to have been chosen by
> my grandmother to be the keeper of our know-
> ledge.... What do we need to do? ... We need to
> go back to ceremony and embrace ceremony as
> part of moving forward. We need to understand
> the laws of our people.

At the same Forum, Elder Stephen Augustine explained the roles of silence and negotiation in Mi'kmaq law. He said silence is a concept, and can be used as a consequence for a wrong action or to teach a lesson. Silence is employed according to proper proced-ures, and ends at a particular time too. Elder Augustine suggested that there is both a place for talking about reconciliation and a need for quiet reflection. Reconciliation cannot occur without listening, contemplation, meditation, and deeper internal deliberation. Silence in the face of residential school harms is an appropriate response for many Indigenous peoples. We must enlarge the space for respectful silence in journeying toward reconciliation, particularly for Survivors who regard this as key to healing. There is a place for discussion and negotiation for those who want to move beyond silence. Dialogue and mutual adjustment are significant components of Mi'kmaq law. Elder Augustine suggested that other dimensions of human experience — our relationships with the earth and all living beings — are also relevant in working toward reconciliation. This profound insight is an Indigenous law, which could be applied more generally.

Elder Reg Crowshoe told the Commission that Indigenous peoples' world views, oral history traditions, and practices have much to teach us about how to establish respectful relationships among peoples and with the land and all living things. Learning how to live together in a good way happens through sharing stories and practising reconciliation in our everyday lives.

> When we talk about the concept of reconciliation, I think about some of the stories that I've heard in our culture and stories are important.... These stories are so important as theories but at the same time stories are important to oral cultures. So when we talk about stories, we talk about defining our environment and how we look at authorities that come from the land and how that land, when we talk about our relationship with the land, how we look at forgiveness and reconciliation is so important when we look at it historically.
>
> We have stories in our culture about our superheroes, how we treat each other, stories about how

animals and plants give us authorities and privil-
eges to use plants as healing, but we also have stories about practices. How would we practise reconciliation? How would we practise getting together
to talk about reconciliation in an oral perspective?
And those practices are so important.

As Elder Crowshoe explained further, reconciliation requires
talking, but our conversations must be broader than Canada's
conventional approaches. Reconciliation between Aboriginal and
non-Aboriginal Canadians, from an Aboriginal perspective, also
requires reconciliation with the natural world. If human beings
resolve problems between themselves but continue to destroy the
natural world, then reconciliation remains incomplete. This is a
perspective that we as Commissioners have repeatedly heard: that
reconciliation will never occur unless we are also reconciled with
the earth. Mi'kmaq and other Indigenous laws stress that humans
must journey through life in conversation and negotiation with all
creation. Reciprocity and mutual respect help sustain our survival.
It is this kind of healing and survival that is needed in moving
forward from the residential school experience.

Over the course of its work, the Commission created space for
exploring the meanings and concepts of reconciliation. In public
Sharing Circles at National Events and Community Hearings, we
bore witness to powerful moments of truth sharing and humbling
acts of reconciliation. Many Survivors had never been able to tell
their own families the whole truth of what happened to them in the
schools. At hearings in Regina, Saskatchewan, Elder Kirby Littletent
said, "I never told, I just told my children, my grandchildren I went
to boarding school, that's all. I never shared my experiences."

Many spoke to honour the memory of relatives who have passed
on. Simone, an Inuk Survivor from Chesterfield Inlet, Nunavut, said,

I'm here for my parents — "Did you miss me
when I went away?" "Did you cry for me?" — and
I'm here for my brother, who was a victim, and my
niece at the age of five who suffered a head injury
and never came home, and her parents never had
closure. To this day, they have not found the grave
in Winnipeg. And I'm here for them first, and
that's why I'm making a public statement.

Others talked about the importance of reconciling with family
members, and cautioned that this process is just beginning. Patrick
Etherington, a Survivor from St. Anne's residential school in Fort
Albany, Ontario, walked with his son and others from Cochrane,
Ontario, to the National Event in Winnipeg. He said that the walk
helped him to reconnect with his son, and that he "just wanted
to be here because I feel this process that we are starting, we got a
long ways to go."

We saw the children and grandchildren of Survivors who, in
searching for their own identity and place in the world, found
compassion and gained new respect for their relatives who went to
the schools, once they heard about and began to understand their
experiences. At the Northern National Event in Inuvik, Northwest
Territories, Maxine Lacorne said,

As a youth, a young lady, I talk with people my
age because I have a good understanding. I talk
to people who are residential school Survivors
because I like to hear their stories, you know, and
it gives me more understanding of my parents....
It is an honour to be here, to sit here among
you guys, Survivors. Wow. You guys are strong
people, you guys survived everything. And we're

still going to be here. They tried to take us away.
They tried to take our language away. You guys
are still here, we're still here. I'm still here.

We heard about children whose small acts of everyday resistance
in the face of rampant abuse, neglect, and bullying in the schools
were quite simply heroic. At the TRC British Columbia National
Event, Elder Barney Williams said that "many of us, through our
pain and suffering, managed to hold our heads up ... we were brave
children." We saw old bonds of childhood friendship renewed as
people gathered and found each other at TRC-sponsored events.
Together, they remembered the horrors they had endured even as
they recalled with pride long-forgotten accomplishments in various school sports teams, music, or art activities. We heard from
resilient, courageous Survivors who, despite their traumatic childhood experiences, went on to become influential leaders in their
communities and in all walks of Canadian life, including politics,
government, law, education, medicine, the corporate world, and
the arts.

We heard from officials representing the federal government
that administered the schools. In a Sharing Circle at the Manitoba
National Event, the Honourable Chuck Strahl (then minister of
Indian Affairs and Northern Development Canada) said,

> Governments like to write ... policy, and they like to
> write legislation, and they like to codify things and
> so on. And Aboriginal people want to talk about
> restoration, reconciliation, forgiveness, about heal-
> ing ... about truth. And those things are all things
> of the heart and of relationship, and not of gov-
> ernment policy. Governments do a bad job of that.

Church representatives spoke about their struggles to right the relationship with Aboriginal peoples. In Inuvik, Anglican Archbishop Fred Hiltz told us that

> as a Church, we are renewing our commitment to work with the Assembly of First Nations in addressing long-standing, Indigenous justice issues. As a Church, we are requiring anyone who serves the Church at a national level to go through anti-racism training.... We have a lot to do in our Church to make sure that racism is eliminated.

Educators told us about their growing awareness of the inadequate role that post-secondary institutions played in training the teachers who taught in the schools. They have pledged to change educational practices and curriculum to be more inclusive of Aboriginal knowledge and history. Artists shared their ideas and feelings about truth and reconciliation through songs, paintings, dance, film, and other media. Corporations provided resources to bring Survivors to events, and, in some cases, some of their own staff and managers.

For non-Aboriginal Canadians who came to bear witness to Survivors' life stories, the experience was powerful. One woman said simply, "By listening to your story, my story can change. By listening to your story, I can change."

RECONCILIATION AS RELATIONSHIP

In its 2012 Interim Report, the TRC recommended that federal, provincial, and territorial governments, and all parties to the Settlement Agreement, undertake to meet and explore the *United Nations Declaration on the Rights of Indigenous Peoples*, as a framework for reconciliation in Canada. We remain convinced that the United Nations Declaration provides the necessary principles, norms, and standards for reconciliation to flourish in twenty-first-century Canada.

A reconciliation framework is one in which Canada's political and legal systems, educational and religious institutions, the corporate sector and civic society function in ways that are consistent with the principles set out in the *United Nations Declaration on the Rights of Indigenous Peoples*, which Canada has endorsed. Together, Canadians must do more than just talk about reconciliation; we must learn how to practise reconciliation in our everyday lives — within ourselves and our families, and in our communities, governments, places of worship, schools, and workplaces. To do so constructively, Canadians must remain committed to the ongoing work of establishing and maintaining respectful relationships.

For many Survivors and their families, this commitment is foremost about healing themselves, their communities, and nations, in ways that revitalize individuals as well as Indigenous cultures, languages, spirituality, laws, and governance systems. For governments, building a respectful relationship involves dismantling a centuries-old political and bureaucratic culture in which, all too often, policies and programs are still based on failed notions of assimilation. For churches, demonstrating long-term commitment requires atoning for actions within the residential schools, respecting Indigenous spirituality, and supporting Indigenous peoples' struggles for justice and equity. Schools must teach history in ways that foster mutual respect, empathy, and engagement. All Canadian children and youth deserve to know Canada's honest history, including what happened in the residential schools, and to appreciate the history and knowledge of Indigenous nations who continue to make such a strong contribution to Canada, including our very name and collective identity as a country. For Canadians from all walks of life, reconciliation offers a new way of living together.

5

TRUTH AND RECONCILIATION COMMISSION RECOMMENDATIONS (2015)

CALLS TO ACTION

In order to redress the legacy of residential schools and advance the process of Canadian reconciliation, the Truth and Reconciliation Commission makes the following calls to action.

Legacy

Child Welfare

1. We call upon the federal, provincial, territorial, and Aboriginal governments to commit to reducing the number of Aboriginal children in care by:

   i. Monitoring and assessing neglect investigations.

    ii. Providing adequate resources to enable Aboriginal communities and child-welfare organizations to keep Aboriginal families together where it is safe to do so, and to keep children in culturally appropriate environments, regardless of where they reside.

    iii. Ensuring that social workers and others who conduct child-welfare investigations are properly educated and trained about the history and impacts of residential schools.

    iv. Ensuring that social workers and others who conduct child-welfare investigations are properly educated and trained about the potential for Aboriginal communities and families to provide more appropriate solutions to family healing.

    v. Requiring that all child-welfare decision makers consider the impact of the residential school experience on children and their caregivers.

2. We call upon the federal government, in collaboration with the provinces and territories, to prepare and publish annual reports on the number of Aboriginal children (First Nations, Inuit, and Métis) who are in care, compared with non-Aboriginal children, as well as the reasons for apprehension, the total spending on preventive and care services by child-welfare agencies, and the effectiveness of various interventions.

3. We call upon all levels of government to fully implement Jordan's Principle.

4. We call upon the federal government to enact Aboriginal child-welfare legislation that establishes national standards for Aboriginal child apprehension and custody cases and includes principles that:

   i.   Affirm the right of Aboriginal governments to establish and maintain their own child-welfare agencies.
   ii. Require all child-welfare agencies and courts to take the residential school legacy into account in their decision making.
   iii. Establish, as an important priority, a requirement that placements of Aboriginal children into temporary and permanent care be culturally appropriate.

5. We call upon the federal, provincial, territorial, and Aboriginal governments to develop culturally appropriate parenting programs for Aboriginal families.

Education

6. We call upon the Government of Canada to repeal Section 43 of the *Criminal Code of Canada*.

7. We call upon the federal government to develop with Aboriginal groups a joint strategy to eliminate educational and employment gaps between Aboriginal and non-Aboriginal Canadians.

8. We call upon the federal government to eliminate

the discrepancy in federal education funding for First Nations children being educated on reserves and those First Nations children being educated off reserves.

9. We call upon the federal government to prepare and publish annual reports comparing funding for the education of First Nations children on and off reserves, as well as educational and income attainments of Aboriginal peoples in Canada compared with non-Aboriginal people.

10. We call on the federal government to draft new Aboriginal education legislation with the full participation and informed consent of Aboriginal peoples. The new legislation would include a commitment to sufficient funding and would incorporate the following principles:

   i.   Providing sufficient funding to close identified educational achievement gaps within one generation.
   ii. Improving education attainment levels and success rates.
   iii. Developing culturally appropriate curricula.
   iv. Protecting the right to Aboriginal languages, including the teaching of Aboriginal languages as credit courses.
   v.   Enabling parental and community responsibility, control, and accountability, similar to what parents enjoy in public school systems.

    vi. Enabling parents to fully participate in the education of their children.

    vii. Respecting and honouring Treaty relationships.

11. We call upon the federal government to provide adequate funding to end the backlog of First Nations students seeking a post-secondary education.

12. We call upon the federal, provincial, territorial, and Aboriginal governments to develop culturally appropriate early childhood education programs for Aboriginal families.

Language and Culture

13. We call upon the federal government to acknowledge that Aboriginal rights include Aboriginal language rights.

14. We call upon the federal government to enact an Aboriginal Languages Act that incorporates the following principles:

    i. Aboriginal languages are a fundamental and valued element of Canadian culture and society, and there is an urgency to preserve them.

    ii. Aboriginal language rights are reinforced by the Treaties.

    iii. The federal government has a responsibility

to provide sufficient funds for Aboriginal-
language revitalization and preservation.

iv. The preservation, revitalization, and
strengthening of Aboriginal languages and
cultures are best managed by Aboriginal
people and communities.

v. Funding for Aboriginal language initiatives
must reflect the diversity of Aboriginal
languages.

15. We call upon the federal government to appoint, in
consultation with Aboriginal groups, an Aboriginal
Languages Commissioner. The commissioner should
help promote Aboriginal languages and report on the
adequacy of federal funding of Aboriginal-languages
initiatives.

16. We call upon post-secondary institutions to create
university and college degree and diploma programs
in Aboriginal languages.

17. We call upon all levels of government to enable residential school Survivors and their families to reclaim
names changed by the residential school system by
waiving administrative costs for a period of five years
for the name-change process and the revision of official identity documents, such as birth certificates,
passports, driver's licences, health cards, status cards,
and social insurance numbers.

Health

18. We call upon the federal, provincial, territorial, and Aboriginal governments to acknowledge that the current state of Aboriginal health in Canada is a direct result of previous Canadian government policies, including residential schools, and to recognize and implement the health-care rights of Aboriginal people as identified in international law, constitutional law, and under the Treaties.

19. We call upon the federal government, in consultation with Aboriginal peoples, to establish measurable goals to identify and close the gaps in health outcomes between Aboriginal and non-Aboriginal communities, and to publish annual progress reports and assess long-term trends. Such efforts would focus on indicators such as: infant mortality, maternal health, suicide, mental health, addictions, life expectancy, birth rates, infant and child health issues, chronic diseases, illness and injury incidence, and the availability of appropriate health services.

20. In order to address the jurisdictional disputes concerning Aboriginal people who do not reside on reserves, we call upon the federal government to recognize, respect, and address the distinct health needs of the Métis, Inuit, and off-reserve Aboriginal peoples.

21. We call upon the federal government to provide sustainable funding for existing and new Aboriginal healing centres to address the physical, mental,

emotional, and spiritual harms caused by residential schools, and to ensure that the funding of healing centres in Nunavut and the Northwest Territories is a priority.

22. We call upon those who can effect change within the Canadian health-care system to recognize the value of Aboriginal healing practices and use them in the treatment of Aboriginal patients in collaboration with Aboriginal healers and Elders where requested by Aboriginal patients.

23. We call upon all levels of government to:

    i.   Increase the number of Aboriginal professionals working in the health-care field.
    ii. Ensure the retention of Aboriginal health-care providers in Aboriginal communities.
    iii. Provide cultural competency training for all health-care professionals.

24. We call upon medical and nursing schools in Canada to require all students to take a course dealing with Aboriginal health issues, including the history and legacy of residential schools, the *United Nations Declaration on the Rights of Indigenous Peoples*, Treaties and Aboriginal rights, and Indigenous teachings and practices. This will require skills-based training in inter-cultural competency, conflict resolution, human rights, and anti-racism.

Justice

25. We call upon the federal government to establish a written policy that reaffirms the independence of the Royal Canadian Mounted Police to investigate crimes in which the government has its own interest as a potential or real party in civil litigation.

26. We call upon the federal, provincial, and territorial governments to review and amend their respective statutes of limitations to ensure that they conform to the principle that governments and other entities cannot rely on limitation defences to defend legal actions of historical abuse brought by Aboriginal people.

27. We call upon the Federation of Law Societies of Canada to ensure that lawyers receive appropriate cultural competency training, which includes the history and legacy of residential schools, the *United Nations Declaration on the Rights of Indigenous Peoples*, Treaties and Aboriginal rights, Indigenous law, and Aboriginal-Crown relations. This will require skills-based training in intercultural competency, conflict resolution, human rights, and anti-racism.

28. We call upon law schools in Canada to require all law students to take a course in Aboriginal people and the law, which includes the history and legacy of residential schools, the *United Nations Declaration on the Rights of Indigenous Peoples*, Treaties and Aboriginal rights, Indigenous law, and Aboriginal-Crown relations. This will require skills-based training in

intercultural competency, conflict resolution, human rights, and anti-racism.

29. We call upon the parties and, in particular, the federal government, to work collaboratively with plaintiffs not included in the Indian Residential Schools Settlement Agreement to have disputed legal issues determined expeditiously on an agreed set of facts.

30. We call upon federal, provincial, and territorial governments to commit to eliminating the overrepresentation of Aboriginal people in custody over the next decade, and to issue detailed annual reports that monitor and evaluate progress in doing so.

31. We call upon the federal, provincial, and territorial governments to provide sufficient and stable funding to implement and evaluate community sanctions that will provide realistic alternatives to imprisonment for Aboriginal offenders and respond to the underlying causes of offending.

32. We call upon the federal government to amend the *Criminal Code* to allow trial judges, upon giving reasons, to depart from mandatory minimum sentences and restrictions on the use of conditional sentences.

33. We call upon the federal, provincial, and territorial governments to recognize as a high priority the need to address and prevent Fetal Alcohol Spectrum Disorder (FASD), and to develop, in collaboration with

Aboriginal people, FASD preventive programs that can
be delivered in a culturally appropriate manner.

34. We call upon the governments of Canada, the provinces, and territories to undertake reforms to the
criminal justice system to better address the needs
of offenders with Fetal Alcohol Spectrum Disorder
(FASD), including:

  i.   Providing increased community resources
       and powers for courts to ensure that FASD
       is properly diagnosed, and that appropriate
       community supports are in place for those
       with FASD.
  ii. Enacting statutory exemptions from
       mandatory minimum sentences of
       imprisonment for offenders affected by
       FASD.
  iii. Providing community, correctional, and
       parole resources to maximize the ability of
       people with FASD to live in the community.
  iv. Adopting appropriate evaluation mechanisms
       to measure the effectiveness of such programs
       and ensure community safety.

35. We call upon the federal government to eliminate
barriers to the creation of additional Aboriginal healing lodges within the federal correctional system.

36. We call upon the federal, provincial, and territorial
governments to work with Aboriginal communities
to provide culturally relevant services to inmates on

issues such as substance abuse, family and domestic violence, and overcoming the experience of having been sexually abused.

37. We call upon the federal government to provide more supports for Aboriginal programming in halfway houses and parole services.

38. We call upon the federal, provincial, territorial, and Aboriginal governments to commit to eliminating the overrepresentation of Aboriginal youth in custody over the next decade.

39. We call upon the federal government to develop a national plan to collect and publish data on the criminal victimization of Aboriginal people, including data related to homicide and family violence victimization.

40. We call on all levels of government, in collaboration with Aboriginal people, to create adequately funded and accessible Aboriginal-specific victim programs and services with appropriate evaluation mechanisms.

41. We call upon the federal government, in consultation with Aboriginal organizations, to appoint a public inquiry into the causes of, and remedies for, the disproportionate victimization of Aboriginal women and girls. The inquiry's mandate would include:

   i.   Investigation into missing and murdered Aboriginal women and girls.

    ii.   Links to the intergenerational legacy of
          residential schools.

42. We call upon the federal, provincial, and territorial
governments to commit to the recognition and implementation of Aboriginal justice systems in a manner
consistent with the Treaty and Aboriginal rights of
Aboriginal peoples, the *Constitution Act, 1982*, and the
*United Nations Declaration on the Rights of Indigenous
Peoples*, endorsed by Canada in November 2012.

Reconciliation

Canadian Governments and the United Nations Declaration on the Rights of Indigenous People

43. We call upon federal, provincial, territorial, and muni-
cipal governments to fully adopt and implement the
*United Nations Declaration on the Rights of Indigenous
Peoples* as the framework for reconciliation.

44. We call upon the Government of Canada to develop
a national action plan, strategies, and other concrete
measures to achieve the goals of the *United Nations
Declaration on the Rights of Indigenous Peoples*.

Royal Proclamation and Covenant of Reconciliation

45. We call upon the Government of Canada, on behalf
of all Canadians, to jointly develop with Aboriginal

peoples a Royal Proclamation of Reconciliation to be issued by the Crown. The proclamation would build on the Royal Proclamation of 1763 and the Treaty of Niagara of 1764, and reaffirm the nation-to-nation relationship between Aboriginal peoples and the Crown. The proclamation would include, but not be limited to, the following commitments:

i.   Repudiate concepts used to justify European sovereignty over Indigenous lands and peoples such as the Doctrine of Discovery and *terra nullius*.

ii. Adopt and implement the *United Nations Declaration on the Rights of Indigenous Peoples* as the framework for reconciliation.

iii. Renew or establish Treaty relationships based on principles of mutual recognition, mutual respect, and shared responsibility for maintaining those relationships into the future.

iv. Reconcile Aboriginal and Crown constitutional and legal orders to ensure that Aboriginal peoples are full partners in Confederation, including the recognition and integration of Indigenous laws and legal traditions in negotiation and implementation processes involving Treaties, land claims, and other constructive agreements.

46. We call upon the parties to the Indian Residential Schools Settlement Agreement to develop and sign a

Covenant of Reconciliation that would identify principles for working collaboratively to advance reconciliation in Canadian society, and that would include, but not be limited to:

i. Reaffirmation of the parties' commitment to reconciliation.

ii. Repudiation of concepts used to justify European sovereignty over Indigenous lands and peoples, such as the Doctrine of Discovery and *terra nullius*, and the reformation of laws, governance structures, and policies within their respective institutions that continue to rely on such concepts.

iii. Full adoption and implementation of the *United Nations Declaration on the Rights of Indigenous Peoples* as the framework for reconciliation.

iv. Support for the renewal or establishment of Treaty relationships based on principles of mutual recognition, mutual respect, and shared responsibility for maintaining those relationships into the future.

v. Enabling those excluded from the Settlement Agreement to sign onto the Covenant of Reconciliation.

vi. Enabling additional parties to sign onto the Covenant of Reconciliation.

47. We call upon federal, provincial, territorial, and municipal governments to repudiate concepts used to

justify European sovereignty over Indigenous peoples and lands, such as the Doctrine of Discovery and *terra nullius*, and to reform those laws, government policies, and litigation strategies that continue to rely on such concepts.

Settlement Agreement Parties and the United Nations Declaration on the Rights of Indigenous Peoples

48. We call upon the church parties to the Settlement Agreement, and all other faith groups and inter-faith social justice groups in Canada who have not already done so, to formally adopt and comply with the principles, norms, and standards of the *United Nations Declaration on the Rights of Indigenous Peoples* as a framework for reconciliation. This would include, but not be limited to, the following commitments:

    i.   Ensuring that their institutions, policies, programs, and practices comply with the *United Nations Declaration on the Rights of Indigenous Peoples*.

    ii. Respecting Indigenous peoples' right to self-determination in spiritual matters, including the right to practise, develop, and teach their own spiritual and religious traditions, customs, and ceremonies, consistent with Article 12:1 of the *United Nations Declaration on the Rights of Indigenous Peoples*.

iii. Engaging in ongoing public dialogue and
actions to support the *United Nations
Declaration on the Rights of Indigenous Peoples*.

iv. Issuing a statement, no later than March 31,
2016, from all religious denominations and
faith groups, as to how they will implement
the *United Nations Declaration on the Rights
of Indigenous Peoples*.

49. We call upon all religious denominations and faith
groups who have not already done so to repudiate
concepts used to justify European sovereignty over
Indigenous lands and peoples, such as the Doctrine
of Discovery and *terra nullius*.

Equity for Aboriginal People in the Legal System

50. In keeping with the *United Nations Declaration on the
Rights of Indigenous Peoples*, we call upon the federal
government, in collaboration with Aboriginal organizations, to fund the establishment of Indigenous law insti-
tutes for the development, use, and understanding of
Indigenous laws and access to justice in accordance with
the unique cultures of Aboriginal peoples in Canada.

51. We call upon the Government of Canada, as an obligation of its fiduciary responsibility, to develop a policy
of transparency by publishing legal opinions it develops
and upon which it acts or intends to act, in regard to
the scope and extent of Aboriginal and Treaty rights.

52. We call upon the Government of Canada, provincial and territorial governments, and the courts to adopt the following legal principles:

    i.   Aboriginal title claims are accepted once the Aboriginal claimant has established occupation over a particular territory at a particular point in time.
    ii. Once Aboriginal title has been established, the burden of proving any limitation on any rights arising from the existence of that title shifts to the party asserting such a limitation.

National Council for Reconciliation

53. We call upon the Parliament of Canada, in consultation and collaboration with Aboriginal peoples, to enact legislation to establish a National Council for Reconciliation. The legislation would establish the council as an independent, national, oversight body with membership jointly appointed by the Government of Canada and national Aboriginal organizations, and consisting of Aboriginal and non-Aboriginal members. Its mandate would include, but not be limited to, the following:

    i.   Monitor, evaluate, and report annually to Parliament and the people of Canada on the Government of Canada's post-apology progress on reconciliation to ensure that government accountability for reconciling

the relationship between Aboriginal
peoples and the Crown is maintained in
the coming years.

ii. Monitor, evaluate, and report to
Parliament and the people of Canada on
reconciliation progress across all levels
and sectors of Canadian society, including
the implementation of the Truth and
Reconciliation Commission of Canada's
Calls to Action.

iii. Develop and implement a multi-year
National Action Plan for Reconciliation,
which includes research and policy
development, public education programs,
and resources. Promote public dialogue,
public/private partnerships, and public
initiatives for reconciliation.

54. We call upon the Government of Canada to provide multi-year funding for the National Council
for Reconciliation to ensure that it has the financial, human, and technical resources required to
conduct its work, including the endowment of a
National Reconciliation Trust to advance the cause of
reconciliation.

55. We call upon all levels of government to provide
annual reports or any current data requested by the
National Council for Reconciliation so that it can
report on the progress toward reconciliation. The
reports or data would include, but not be limited to:

i.   The number of Aboriginal children —
     including Métis and Inuit children — in
     care, compared with non-Aboriginal
     children, the reasons for apprehension, and
     the total spending on preventive and care
     services by child-welfare agencies.

ii. Comparative funding for the education of
     First Nations children on and off reserves.

iii. The educational and income attainments
     of Aboriginal peoples in Canada compared
     with non-Aboriginal people.

iv. Progress on closing the gaps between
     Aboriginal and non-Aboriginal communities
     in a number of health indicators such as:
     infant mortality, maternal health, suicide,
     mental health, addictions, life expectancy,
     birth rates, infant and child health
     issues, chronic diseases, illness and injury
     incidence, and the availability of appropriate
     health services.

v.   Progress on eliminating the
     overrepresentation of Aboriginal children in
     youth custody over the next decade.

vi. Progress on reducing the rate of criminal
     victimization of Aboriginal people,
     including data related to homicide and
     family violence victimization and other
     crimes.

vii. Progress on reducing the overrepresentation
     of Aboriginal people in the justice and
     correctional systems.

56. We call upon the prime minister of Canada to formally respond to the report of the National Council for Reconciliation by issuing an annual "State of Aboriginal Peoples" report, which would outline the government's plans for advancing the cause of reconciliation.

Professional Development and Training for Public Servants

57. We call upon federal, provincial, territorial, and municipal governments to provide education to public servants on the history of Aboriginal peoples, including the history and legacy of residential schools, the *United Nations Declaration on the Rights of Indigenous Peoples*, Treaties and Aboriginal rights, Indigenous law, and Aboriginal-Crown relations. This will require skills-based training in intercultural competency, conflict resolution, human rights, and anti-racism.

Church Apologies and Reconciliation

58. We call upon the Pope to issue an apology to Survivors, their families, and communities for the Roman Catholic Church's role in the spiritual, cultural, emotional, physical, and sexual abuse of First Nations, Inuit, and Métis children in Catholic-run residential schools. We call for that apology to be similar to the 2010 apology issued to Irish victims of abuse and to occur within one year of the issuing of this Report and to be delivered by the Pope in Canada.

59. We call upon church parties to the Settlement Agreement to develop ongoing education strategies to ensure that their respective congregations learn about their church's role in colonization, the history and legacy of residential schools, and why apologies to former residential school students, their families, and communities were necessary.

60. We call upon leaders of the church parties to the Settlement Agreement and all other faiths, in collaboration with Indigenous spiritual leaders, Survivors, schools of theology, seminaries, and other religious training centres, to develop and teach curriculum for all student clergy, and all clergy and staff who work in Aboriginal communities, on the need to respect Indigenous spirituality in its own right, the history and legacy of residential schools and the roles of the church parties in that system, the history and legacy of religious conflict in Aboriginal families and communities, and the responsibility that churches have to mitigate such conflicts and prevent spiritual violence.

61. We call upon church parties to the Settlement Agreement, in collaboration with Survivors and representatives of Aboriginal organizations, to establish permanent funding to Aboriginal people for:

    i.   Community-controlled healing and reconciliation projects.
    ii. Community-controlled culture- and language-revitalization projects.

iii. Community-controlled education and relationship-building projects.
iv. Regional dialogues for Indigenous spiritual leaders and youth to discuss Indigenous spirituality, self-determination, and reconciliation.

Education for Reconciliation

62. We call upon the federal, provincial, and territorial governments, in consultation and collaboration with Survivors, Aboriginal peoples, and educators, to:

i. Make age-appropriate curriculum on residential schools, Treaties, and Aboriginal peoples' historical and contemporary contributions to Canada a mandatory education requirement for Kindergarten to Grade Twelve students.
ii. Provide the necessary funding to post-secondary institutions to educate teachers on how to integrate Indigenous knowledge and teaching methods into classrooms.
iii. Provide the necessary funding to Aboriginal schools to utilize Indigenous knowledge and teaching methods in classrooms.
iv. Establish senior-level positions in government at the assistant deputy minister level or higher dedicated to Aboriginal content in education.

63. We call upon the Council of Ministers of Education, Canada, to maintain an annual commitment to Aboriginal education issues, including:

     i.   Developing and implementing Kindergarten to Grade Twelve curriculum and learning resources on Aboriginal peoples in Canadian history, and the history and legacy of residential schools.
     ii. Sharing information and best practices on teaching curriculum related to residential schools and Aboriginal history.
     iii. Building student capacity for intercultural understanding, empathy, and mutual respect.
     iv. Identifying teacher-training needs relating to the above.

64. We call upon all levels of government that provide public funds to denominational schools to require such schools to provide an education on comparative religious studies, which must include a segment on Aboriginal spiritual beliefs and practices developed in collaboration with Aboriginal Elders.

65. We call upon the federal government, through the Social Sciences and Humanities Research Council, and in collaboration with Aboriginal peoples, post-secondary institutions, and educators, and the National Centre for Truth and Reconciliation and its partner institutions, to establish a national research program with multi-year funding to advance understanding of reconciliation.

Youth Programs

66. We call upon the federal government to establish multi-year funding for community-based youth organizations to deliver programs on reconciliation, and establish a national network to share information and best practices.

Museums and Archives

67. We call upon the federal government to provide funding to the Canadian Museums Association to undertake, in collaboration with Aboriginal peoples, a national review of museum policies and best practices to determine the level of compliance with the *United Nations Declaration on the Rights of Indigenous Peoples* and to make recommendations.

68. We call upon the federal government, in collaboration with Aboriginal peoples, and the Canadian Museums Association to mark the 150th anniversary of Canadian Confederation in 2017 by establishing a dedicated national funding program for commemoration projects on the theme of reconciliation.

69. We call upon Library and Archives Canada to:

    i.   Fully adopt and implement the *United Nations Declaration on the Rights of Indigenous Peoples* and the *United Nations*

Joinet-Orentlicher Principles, as related
to Aboriginal peoples' inalienable right
to know the truth about what happened
and why, with regard to human rights
violations committed against them in the
residential schools.

ii. Ensure that its record holdings related to
residential schools are accessible to the
public.

iii. Commit more resources to its public
education materials and programming on
residential schools.

70. We call upon the federal government to provide funding
to the Canadian Association of Archivists to undertake,
in collaboration with Aboriginal peoples, a national
review of archival policies and best practices to:

i. Determine the level of compliance with the
*United Nations Declaration on the Rights of
Indigenous Peoples* and the *United Nations
Joinet-Orentlicher Principles*, as related
to Aboriginal peoples' inalienable right
to know the truth about what happened
and why, with regard to human rights
violations committed against them in the
residential schools.

ii. Produce a report with recommendations for
full implementation of these international
mechanisms as a reconciliation framework
for Canadian archives.

Missing Children and Burial Information

71. We call upon all chief coroners and provincial vital statistics agencies that have not provided to the Truth and Reconciliation Commission of Canada their records on the deaths of Aboriginal children in the care of residential school authorities to make these documents available to the National Centre for Truth and Reconciliation.

72. We call upon the federal government to allocate sufficient resources to the National Centre for Truth and Reconciliation to allow it to develop and maintain the National Residential School Student Death Register established by the Truth and Reconciliation Commission of Canada.

73. We call upon the federal government to work with churches, Aboriginal communities, and former residential school students to establish and maintain an online registry of residential school cemeteries, including, where possible, plot maps showing the location of deceased residential school children.

74. We call upon the federal government to work with the churches and Aboriginal community leaders to inform the families of children who died at residential schools of the child's burial location, and to respond to families' wishes for appropriate commemoration ceremonies and markers, and reburial in home communities where requested.

75. We call upon the federal government to work with provincial, territorial, and municipal governments, churches, Aboriginal communities, former residential school students, and current landowners to develop and implement strategies and procedures for the ongoing identification, documentation, maintenance, commemoration, and protection of residential school cemeteries or other sites at which residential school children were buried. This is to include the provision of appropriate memorial ceremonies and commemorative markers to honour the deceased children.

76. We call upon the parties engaged in the work of documenting, maintaining, commemorating, and protecting residential school cemeteries to adopt strategies in accordance with the following principles:

    i.   The Aboriginal community most affected shall lead the development of such strategies.
    ii. Information shall be sought from residential school Survivors and other Knowledge Keepers in the development of such strategies.
    iii. Aboriginal protocols shall be respected before any potentially invasive technical inspection and investigation of a cemetery site.

National Centre for Truth and Reconciliation

77. We call upon provincial, territorial, municipal, and community archives to work collaboratively with the National Centre for Truth and Reconciliation to

identify and collect copies of all records relevant to
the history and legacy of the residential school system, and to provide these to the National Centre for
Truth and Reconciliation.

78. We call upon the Government of Canada to commit to making a funding contribution of $10 million
over seven years to the National Centre for Truth and
Reconciliation, plus an additional amount to assist
communities to research and produce histories of their
own residential school experience and their involvement in truth, healing, and reconciliation.

Commemoration

79. We call upon the federal government, in collaboration
with Survivors, Aboriginal organizations, and the arts
community, to develop a reconciliation framework for
Canadian heritage and commemoration. This would
include, but not be limited to:

  i. Amending the Historic Sites and Monuments
      Act to include First Nations, Inuit, and
      Métis representation on the Historic Sites
      and Monuments Board of Canada and its
      Secretariat.
  ii. Revising the policies, criteria, and practices
      of the National Program of Historical
      Commemoration to integrate Indigenous
      history, heritage values, and memory practices
      into Canada's national heritage and history.

iii. Developing and implementing a national
heritage plan and strategy for commemorating
residential school sites, the history and legacy
of residential schools, and the contributions
of Aboriginal peoples to Canada's history.

80. We call upon the federal government, in collaboration
with Aboriginal peoples, to establish, as a statutory
holiday, a National Day for Truth and Reconciliation
to honour Survivors, their families, and communities,
and ensure that public commemoration of the history
and legacy of residential schools remains a vital component of the reconciliation process.

81. We call upon the federal government, in collaboration
with Survivors and their organizations, and other parties to the Settlement Agreement, to commission and
install a publicly accessible, highly visible, Residential
Schools National Monument in the city of Ottawa to
honour Survivors and all the children who were lost
to their families and communities.

82. We call upon provincial and territorial governments,
in collaboration with Survivors and their organizations, and other parties to the Settlement Agreement,
to commission and install a publicly accessible, highly
visible, Residential Schools Monument in each cap-
ital city to honour Survivors and all the children who
were lost to their families and communities.

83. We call upon the Canada Council for the Arts to establish, as a funding priority, a strategy for Indigenous

and non-Indigenous artists to undertake collaborative projects and produce works that contribute to the reconciliation process.

Media and Reconciliation

84. We call upon the federal government to restore and increase funding to the CBC/Radio-Canada, to enable Canada's national public broadcaster to support reconciliation, and be properly reflective of the diverse cultures, languages, and perspectives of Aboriginal peoples, including, but not limited to:

   i. Increasing Aboriginal programming, including Aboriginal-language speakers.
   ii. Increasing equitable access for Aboriginal peoples to jobs, leadership positions, and professional development opportunities within the organization.
   iii. Continuing to provide dedicated news coverage and online public information resources on issues of concern to Aboriginal peoples and all Canadians, including the history and legacy of residential schools and the reconciliation process.

85. We call upon the Aboriginal Peoples Television Network, as an independent non-profit broadcaster with programming by, for, and about Aboriginal peoples, to support reconciliation, including but not limited to:

      i.   Continuing to provide leadership in programming and organizational culture that reflects the diverse cultures, languages, and perspectives of Aboriginal peoples.

     ii.   Continuing to develop media initiatives that inform and educate the Canadian public, and connect Aboriginal and non-Aboriginal Canadians.

86. We call upon Canadian journalism programs and media schools to require education for all students on the history of Aboriginal peoples, including the history and legacy of residential schools, the *United Nations Declaration on the Rights of Indigenous Peoples*, Treaties and Aboriginal rights, Indigenous law, and Aboriginal-Crown relations.

Sports and Reconciliation

87. We call upon all levels of government, in collaboration with Aboriginal peoples, sports halls of fame, and other relevant organizations, to provide public education that tells the national story of Aboriginal athletes in history.

88. We call upon all levels of government to take action to ensure long-term Aboriginal athlete development and growth, and continued support for the North American Indigenous Games, including funding to host the games and for provincial and territorial team preparation and travel.

89. We call upon the federal government to amend the Physical Activity and Sport Act to support reconciliation by ensuring that policies to promote physical activity as a fundamental element of health and well-being, reduce barriers to sports participation, increase the pursuit of excellence in sport, and build capacity in the Canadian sport system, are inclusive of Aboriginal peoples.

90. We call upon the federal government to ensure that national sports policies, programs, and initiatives are inclusive of Aboriginal peoples, including, but not limited to, establishing:

    i.   In collaboration with provincial and territorial governments, stable funding for, and access to, community sports programs that reflect the diverse cultures and traditional sporting activities of Aboriginal peoples.
    ii. An elite athlete development program for Aboriginal athletes.
    iii. Programs for coaches, trainers, and sports officials that are culturally relevant for Aboriginal peoples.
    iv. Anti-racism awareness and training programs.

91. We call upon the officials and host countries of international sporting events such as the Olympics, Pan Am, and Commonwealth games to ensure that Indigenous peoples' territorial protocols are respected, and local Indigenous communities are engaged in all aspects of planning and participating in such events.

Business and Reconciliation

92. We call upon the corporate sector in Canada to adopt the *United Nations Declaration on the Rights of Indigenous Peoples* as a reconciliation framework and to apply its principles, norms, and standards to corporate policy and core operational activities involving Indigenous peoples and their lands and resources. This would include, but not be limited to, the following:

    i.   Commit to meaningful consultation, building respectful relationships, and obtaining the free, prior, and informed consent of Indigenous peoples before proceeding with economic development projects.

    ii. Ensure that Aboriginal peoples have equitable access to jobs, training, and education opportunities in the corporate sector, and that Aboriginal communities gain long-term sustainable benefits from economic development projects.

    iii. Provide education for management and staff on the history of Aboriginal peoples, including the history and legacy of residential schools, the *United Nations Declaration on the Rights of Indigenous Peoples*, Treaties and Aboriginal rights, Indigenous law, and Aboriginal-Crown relations. This will require skills based training in intercultural competency, conflict resolution, human rights, and anti-racism.

Newcomers to Canada

93. We call upon the federal government, in collaboration with the national Aboriginal organizations, to revise the information kit for newcomers to Canada and its citizenship test to reflect a more inclusive history of the diverse Aboriginal peoples of Canada, including information about the Treaties and the history of residential schools.

94. We call upon the government of Canada to replace the Oath of Citizenship with the following:

   I swear (or affirm) that I will be faithful and bear true allegiance to Her Majesty Queen Elizabeth II, Queen of Canada, Her Heirs and Successors, and that I will faithfully observe the laws of Canada including Treaties with Indigenous Peoples, and fulfill my duties as a Canadian citizen.

ACKNOWLEDGEMENTS

The author would like to thank his wife, Marie-Jeanne, and son, Alain, as well as Bob Blackburn, Garry Smith, and John Graham for reading and offering comments on the manuscript. Thank you also to the staff at Dundurn, Publisher and President Kirk Howard, and Editor-at-Large Patrick Boyer for their encouragement and support.